GUEST OF HONOR
AT A NECKTIE PARTY . . .

Cuchillo knocked the gun from Likes Horses' hand. He was about to strike her again when Likes Horses leaped to her feet and raced into the woods.

Sanchez and one of the other men started to go after her. But Camargo halted them by holding up his hand. "Let her go. We'll catch up with her. But first—hang him high, Cuchillo."

The Indian, beginning to grin, tied the end of the rope to the trunk of the tree. As Gabe raised his head to get one last glimpse of the blue sky above him, Cuchillo slapped the bay's rump. The horse let out an explosive snort then broke into a gallop.

Gabe was pulled from the saddle. His body swung back and forth at the end of the rope. As his air supply was cut off, a fire hotter than any he had ever known began to burn in his lungs. . . .

Also in the LONG RIDER Series

LONG RIDER

THE COMANCHEROS

CLAY DAWSON

14

DIAMOND BOOKS, NEW YORK

THE COMANCHEROS

A Diamond Book / published by arrangement with
the author

PRINTING HISTORY
Diamond edition / March 1991

ISBN: 1–55773–480–1

Diamond Books are published by The Berkley Publishing
Group, 200 Madison Avenue, New York, New York 10016.
The name "DIAMOND" and its logo are trademarks
belonging to Charter Communications, Inc.

PRINTED IN THE UNITED STATES OF AMERICA

10 9 8 7 6 5 4 3 2 1

THE COMANCHEROS

CHAPTER ONE

Rain.

It fell in torrents. Sheets of it—thick gray masses—swept across Texas' Stockton Plateau, driven by a wild wind that tore down out of the Davis Mountains to the west and went wailing across the hilly land.

The rain lashed the lean body and rawboned face of the lone rider aboard a roan gelding as he made his way with head bent and shoulders hunched toward the distant mountains, which were barely visible to him because of the blinding rain.

The rain fell in under the turned-up canvas collar of his yellow slicker, pelting the rest of it where it was spread out over the rump of his roan, and poured from the down-tilted brim of his black Stetson. It seemed determined to turn the world to water.

The rider moved on, feeling the uneven gait of the roan as its hooves sank in the muddy bog the land had become because of the deluge. He swayed slightly in the saddle as the horse plodded on, lurching first to one side then to the other as it struggled to pull its hooves out of the grasping mud. Around him cedars and Spanish oaks occasionally came into blurry view, their soaked branches hanging down in mute defeat beneath the rain's relentless onslaught.

He sat his saddle determinedly, stoically, pushing himself and his horse on as if the rain made no difference to him. His tall body, as slender as it was strong, was relaxed but not indolent, and although there was no tension in it, there was a readiness to move and move fast if action became necessary. His ghost-gray eyes were alert but not uneasy; they took in the wet world around him in a kind of wary record keeping. They saw both the good and the bad. Nothing escaped their notice. The rider's hair was the color of a streambed's sand and had not known a barber's touch in some time. It buried the rider's ears and the nape of his neck. His hands were large and long fingered, and could gently caress the face and body of a woman as easily as they could kill in a situation where killing was called for. The index finger on his right hand was badly bent as a result of having been broken in a fistfight in the distant past, and since then was useless as a trigger finger. For this reason, the .44 caliber Frontier model Colt in the holster he wore on his right hip had its butt facing forward to allow for a fast cross-draw with his left hand. The weapon used the same .44-40 ammunition as did the Winchester securely housed in his saddle scabbard.

His eyes caught the swift flash of lightning that seared the sky above his head, so he was prepared for the thunder that followed. It cannonaded through the land, causing his horse to shudder. He tightened his grip on the reins to keep the horse from bolting as another spear of lightning soared across the sky and another bolt of thunder rumbled through the rain.

The roan tossed its head, fighting the bit. It high-stepped, its great eyes rolling, its water-soaked mane flying.

"Easy," the rider said. He reached out and stroked his mount's neck. "Nice and easy, that's the way to take it," he practically purred, just loud enough to be heard above the sound of the falling rain. His hand slid smoothly along the animal's tense neck. Within moments, he felt the horse begin to relax. Its flesh no longer rippled nervously under his touch. It seemed instead to welcome the warmth of the gentling hand. It nickered.

"I know. We're having about as much fun as a baby with a bellyache. But the rain'll end. It's just a question of when."

The rider's name was Gabe Conrad. Once upon a long-ago time his name had been Long Rider, when he had lived among the Oglala Sioux. He had spent most of his childhood among the Oglalas, together with his mother, after they had both been taken captive by the Indians. The name Long Rider had become his as a result of a long and grueling ride he'd made, during which two horses had died under him as he rode to warn a Sioux village of an impending attack by the United States Army. That ride had been made when he was fourteen years old. It brought him fame among the People—as the Sioux called themselves—and had made him a legend among them.

He drew rein and stepped down from the saddle onto the boggy ground to give his horse a rest. It was tough traveling over such unstable ground, he knew. No use making it more difficult for the roan by forcing it to bear the weight of a rider. He began to walk, leading the horse. The animal, as if grateful for the consideration being shown it, nuzzled its master's neck.

Man and horse walked on through the rain, their heads bent, their boots and hooves sinking into the waterlogged ground. All around them grew lush stands of bluestem and buffalo grasses, except in those areas that had been clearly overgrazed.

Gabe hardly heard the thunder that continued to boom around him. He was listening to the thunder that rumbled in his gut and bore testimony to his growing hunger. He hadn't eaten in more than fifteen hours, he estimated. Not since he had stopped back along the trail and dug some sego lily bulbs from the ground, which he had then roasted. Now he wanted meat. But he knew he had little or no chance of getting any until the storm ended, because game went to ground when it rained.

He looked up at the sky. Dark. Almost black.

Rain flooded his eyes. He blinked it away and looked down at the ground, a defensive measure. He walked on, no longer having to lead his horse, which now walked by his side.

An hour later, the lightning died. So did the thunder. But the rain continued, although with less force. Half an hour after that, it slowed and finally stopped altogether. As water dripped from the trees and gullied down the sides of hills, the storm clouds began to crumble and soon there were patches of blue between them. When the sun reappeared, the summer storm faded to only a memory.

Gabe climbed back into the saddle and then took off his slicker. He folded it and, reaching behind him, stuffed it into one of his saddlebags. He basked in the warmth of the sun as he rode on and his shirt, which had been dampened by rain that had found its way under his collar, began to dry. He kept his eyes on the ground as he searched for sign of any animal that might become a meal. But none was to be seen as a result of the rain. Tracks and even scat, if there had been any in the area, had been washed away or buried in the mud.

He looked up at the branches of the trees he passed. It wasn't long before his keen eyes spotted a squirrel's nest that was composed of pieces of bark, leaves and small branches. It sat some thirty feet above the ground on a thick branch of pine not far from the tree's trunk. Gabe scanned the area beneath the tree and noted pinecones littering the ground beneath the nest, all of which had been nibbled, which meant that the nest was inhabited. Probably the home of a female who had spent the spring raising a brood.

He drew rein and watched the nest. All around it drops of rainwater dripped from leaves. The drops grew, became fat, caught the sunlight, refracted it into jewel-like colors—red, green, yellow—and then fell. The fleeting treasures of *wi*, thought Gabe, using the Sioux name for the sun, one of the People's four superior spirits. *Wi*, he thought, makes jewels out of water and light, and *tate*, the wind, scatters them.

His eyes caught movement in the distance. Something was moving through the tobosa grass. He watched the movement of the grass and realized that the animal hidden in the tobosa was moving in a nearly straight line toward the pine tree that harbored the nest. He drew his Colt and cocked it. As he did so, a squirrel emerged from the tobosa grass at the base of the pine and scampered up the tree's trunk.

It never reached its nest. Gabe's first shot brought it down.

He holstered his gun and rode over to where his quarry lay at the base of the pine tree and dismounted. After picking up the dead squirrel, he led his horse into a small grove of pines and shin oaks. When he reached the middle of the grove, he left his horse ground-hitched and proceeded to break off several branches of a shin oak sapling. He hunkered down and, taking a tin container of wooden matches from a pocket of his jeans, set about building a cookfire. It was no easy task. The wood, wet from the rain, was slow to ignite and, once ignited, was slower to burn as well as smoky.

The smoke made Gabe uneasy. It would signal his presence in the grove to anyone else who might be in the area. He looked up and was pleased to see that most of the thick smoke was dissipating in the branches of the trees, which was why he had chosen the grove rather than open country for his campsite.

When the fire, although sputtering and occasionally threatening to go out entirely, was burning brightly, Gabe withdrew the knife from the scabbard sewn to the outside of his side arm's holster. He used its blade to incise the squirrel's hind legs, then to pull the skin of the legs up toward the body. He inserted a finger into the broken skin at one hip and pulled hard. He turned the squirrel over and repeated the process, stripping away all the skin except for a small patch over the animal's genitals. Grasping both hind legs in one hand, he used his other hand to pull the skin up toward the head. He had skinned all of the animal except for part of the front legs, which he peeled until the skin tore away, leaving only a small piece of fur behind. One final pull and he had the squirrel's hide over its head. With one deft slice he severed the squirrel's head and its covering hide, which he tossed aside. Then he cut off the feet and tail.

He found a reasonably flat rock and placed the skinned squirrel on its back on the rock. He made an abdominal cut from tail to throat and then cut through the pelvic bone, separating the hips. He used his knife to open the rib cage and removed the internal organs by pulling them through the pelvic area along with the genitals and anus, which he had been careful not to cut into while dressing his kill. He rose and carried the carcass to a puddle that had formed during the rainstorm on the concave surface of a nearby boulder. He dunked the carcass in the water to cleanse it of any remaining blood and intestinal fluids. Leaving the carcass in the water to cool it somewhat before cooking it, he returned to the fire and cut two crotched sticks from his woodpile, which he placed upright on either side of the fire. Cutting another stick, he carried it back to the shallow pool of water in which the skinned body of the squirrel lay soaking and used it to spear the animal. Back at the fire, he laid the stick that held the carcass in the crotches of the two uprights and slowly began to turn it.

There was little fat on the carcass, but what there was sizzled as it bubbled and fell into the flames below. Gabe's mouth watered as he continued turning the spit, and the carcass began to turn tan and, after a time, brown. He continued turning the spit until he was reasonably sure that the meat had been cooked all the way through. To make sure that it had been, he poked it with the end of a stick, one end of which he had whittled into a sharp point. The stick easily entered the meat.

Gabe removed the spit from the crotched uprights and, holding its ends in both hands, he began to eat. Although the meat was hot and burned his tongue, his hunger ruled and he continued tearing into the roasted flesh with his teeth. It had a strong gamy flavor; the meal would have benefited from having been cooled for a longer period of time to diminish that pungent flavor, which was the result of retained body heat. Gabe nevertheless found the meal not merely tasty but almost delicious.

He broke off the meat and gnawed it from the bones before tossing them aside. He spat bits of gristle into the flames. His meal's juices stained his lips and chin.

Soon, the meat was gone.

But so was Gabe's hunger. He dropped the spit, wiped his lips and chin with the back of his hand, and got up. He opened the canteen that hung from his saddle horn and took a deep drink of water. Then he went back to the fire, sat down with his back braced against the trunk of a pine and, with his forearms resting on his upright knees, closed his eyes and listened to the silence that surrounded him.

Listened to what a white man would call the silence surrounding him. But Gabe, though his skin was white, was not, by either experience or training, altogether a white man. He was more Indian than white. Where a white man would hear only silence, he heard *tate* passing through the branches of the trees above his head, the wind's passage an almost inaudible echo of a whisper. He heard the sound of a beetle scurrying through some fallen pine needles. He heard the *tap-tap-tap* of one branch lightly brushing another one a good twenty yards away.

His eyes closed, his hunger satisfied, his heart light— Gabe was content. He heard a faint *whooshing* sound and knew that an owl had just journeyed above his head. He heard a fox bark in the distance. Both the owl and the fox were hunting what they needed to sustain them for another day, another night. As I have just done, Gabe thought. He said a silent prayer of thanks to *Yumni,* one of the People's sacred spirits.

In the darkness behind his closed eyes, Gabe saw a gigantic version of a wheel of fortune he had once seen at a county fair in Missouri. But this one was not spun by a mortal man as that one had been, but by *Yumni,* and all men played at the spirit of games' urging—they could not refuse to play by virtue of merely having been born—and those who won turned to the right and the light, while those who lost turned to the left and darkness, and the horrors that the darkness held.

The sounds his roan made as it browsed the brush beneath the trees broke into Gabe's reverie. He opened his eyes and got up. By the angle of the sunlight filtering through the trees to dapple the ground around him, he knew that the sun was well on its way to the horizon. He estimated that there were still two hours or so of daylight left. Time enough to cover more miles before making camp for the night. He went to the fire and stomped it out, sending a fiery shower of sparks up into the air.

Then he went to his horse and, after stepping into the saddle, rode out of the grove, heading west toward the Pecos River and the Davis Mountains beyond it.

He heard the riders before he saw them. The sound of pounding hooves was loud in the otherwise quiet land, but he could not see them or their mounts because of the rolling hill country through which he rode. He headed for the cover of a hummock a few yards ahead of him. Cresting it, he looked around but still saw no riders, though the sound of their mounts traveling in his direction was louder now. He rode down the far side of the hummock and dismounted. Leaving his horse ground-hitched and with his hand on his six-gun, he bellied down on the ground. Taking off his hat, he peered cautiously over the top of the hummock at the series of small hills and shallow valleys through which he had been traveling.

There!

Straight ahead and a little to the north. Five riders. One well out in front, four behind. All of them Indians. The man out front was a Comanche; the other four were Apaches. All of them were riding as if the Devil himself was on their backtrail. The four Apaches were trying to narrow the distance between themselves and the Comanche, who was obviously fleeing from them.

Gabe saw blood on the face of the Comanche. He saw the man's horse falter and almost fall. Four against one. Bad odds. He decided to alter them. He rose, clapped his hat back on his head and swung into the saddle. Turning his horse, he crested the hummock and rode down it, heading for the Indians who were all heading in his direction.

One of the four Apaches let out a whoop when he caught sight of Gabe, and then brandished the bow he held in his right hand. The other three acknowledged Gabe's presence with whoops of their own as they pounded on in pursuit of their prey.

Gabe, as he rode, drew his Winchester from his saddle scabbard. Dropping his reins, he raised the weapon and squeezed off a shot that angled its way in front of the four pursuers. It did nothing to slow them down. He fired again, the round traveling closer to the four Apaches this time, almost close enough to nick the nostrils of the lead rider's horse.

Whoops of rage went up from the four, and one of them swerved toward Gabe and threw a feathered lance at him.

Gabe sharply turned his horse as the lance arced down to strike the ground where he had been only moments before. The lance quivered with the force of impact and then was still. Its owner headed for it. As he passed Gabe at a distance of some forty yards, Gabe fired, and his round split the shaft of the lance just inches above the point where it emerged from the ground.

The Apache whose lance had just been rendered useless let out a roar of rage, veered sharply, and headed for Gabe, drawing an arrow from his quiver and his bow from his shoulder. But he slowed his horse and then turned and fled when Gabe raised his rifle with deliberate speed and took aim at him.

Gabe slammed his spurs into his horse's flanks then and galloped after the other three Apaches, who were still in pursuit of the Comanche with the bloodied face.

They heard him coming, but before they could react to his headlong pursuit Gabe had caught up with them and ridden in between two of them. Holding his rifle by its barrel now, he swung it in a wide arc. Down from his horse went the Apache on his right. The Apache riding on his left let out a shriek as the rifle stock struck him on the shoulder, but he didn't go down—not until Gabe brought the rifle back, retracing its violent arc. This time the gun's stock slammed into the skull of the Apache on the left and sent him flying out of the saddle to land with a bone-jarring thud on the ground.

The remaining Apache had wheeled his horse and was heading back toward Gabe, his quarry forgotten, the war club in his hand raised high above his head.

Gabe had no time to get out of the man's way, so he swung his left leg over his saddle horn and leaped to the ground, his rifle still in his hand.

He had no sooner done so than the Apache's war club landed with a bone-crunching blow on his saddle. The blow brought the roan to its knees. The horse rolled over, stirrups flying and dust rising around it, and then got shakily to its feet as the Apache circled around and headed back toward Gabe.

Gabe dropped to one knee and raised his Winchester.

His round shattered the Apache's raised war club, sending splinters of wood flying in every direction.

The man threw away what remained of his war club and leaped from his horse, landing on top of Gabe to bring him down and sent his rifle skittering across the ground.

Gabe squirmed out from under the man, whose greasy

body reeked, and kicked him in the shin before leaping to his feet. The kick seemed to have no effect on the Apache. He too sprang to his feet and drew a knife that hung in a scabbard from his belt. He lunged with his knife slashing upward in an effort to gut Gabe.

But Gabe, bending his body in the middle, managed to avoid the knife's razor edge. He reached out then with both hands and seized the wrist of the man's knife hand, twisting it and forcing him to drop his weapon. Then, as the Apache tried to gouge out Gabe's right eye with the thumb of his free hand, Gabe ripped off the red cloth headband the Apache had been wearing. Spinning him around so that the Indian's back was to him, Gabe gripped the headband in both hands and looped it over the man's head and down around his neck. He swiftly drew the headband taut.

The Apache clawed at it but to no avail. He twisted and turned as choked grunts escaped from his throat. He continued his desperate attempts to free himself as he began to gasp for air. Then, as if poleaxed, he went limp.

Gabe let go of the headband and the Apache crumpled to the ground in an unconscious heap, but Gabe had no time to savor his triumph. The other two Apaches he had unhorsed were racing toward him. Both men's thin lips were twisted in silent snarls and their eyes blazed with anger. Both men had knives in their hands.

Gabe quickly backed up and drew his Colt. "Hold it!" he yelled, and then, *"Stop!"*

Neither Apache obeyed his shouted commands, either because they had not understood or because they had chosen to ignore them. Gabe fired a warning shot that kicked up dust in front of the oncoming men.

They slowed.

He fired a second shot.

They halted and stepped backward, the fading sunlight glinting on the blades of their knives.

He took a step in their direction.

One of the Apaches threw his knife.

It cut through Gabe's shirt and sliced his left bicep before falling to the ground. Gabe let out a howl fueled by fury and fired a snap shot that caught the knife-thrower in the throat, lifting him off the ground and turning him around to fall, with blood spurting in a crimson geyser from his throat, to the ground with outstretched arms. He lay there twitching as his companion stared down at him and Gabe thumbed back the hammer of his gun.

The loud *click* caught the second Apache's attention. He glanced at Gabe, dropped his knife and lunged.

Before Gabe could fire, an arrow flew through the air and buried itself in the man's chest. He gagged, both of his hands flying up to grip the arrow's shaft. He was holding on to it, his eyes squeezed shut in agony, when a second arrow followed the first and slammed into his gut, doubling him over.

Gabe glanced over his shoulder and saw the Comanche who had been pursued by the Apaches sitting his saddle and drawing back his bowstring. As he released another arrow and the bowstring twanged, Gabe turned his head and saw the third arrow enter the chest of the Apache, who made no sound as his knees buckled and he went down, his eyes empty as death claimed him.

The other Apache, whom Gabe had rendered unconscious with the man's own headband, was getting groggily to his feet. He stood there, swaying and staring at his two dead companions, then turned and ran. Gabe and the Comanche watched him leap onto the bare back of his horse and, gripping the animal's mane, send it galloping in the same direction the fourth Apache had fled in when Gabe had first drawn his gun. In moments, the man had disappeared over the top of a hill.

Gabe went to where his Winchester lay on the ground. He picked it up, carried it over to where his horse stood and thrust it into his saddle scabbard. Then, turning to the mounted Comanche, he said, "I thank you kindly for killing that man before he could kill me."

"It is you I must thank," responded the Comanche. "What I wonder is why?"

"I don't follow you."

"You—a white man—"

"Being white's got nothing whatsoever to do with it," Gabe interrupted, "if you're talking about how I lent you a hand just now. What mattered was the bad odds of four men against one."

The Comanche frowned, obviously puzzled.

"Four against one, that's not exactly fair. What's more it's downright dangerous—for the one." A faint smile ghosted across his face.

The Comanche matched his smile.

Gabe turned to his horse. He gripped the reins and led the animal around in a circle to see if the blow from the marauding Apache's war club had done any permanent damage.

The roan limped slightly but almost unnoticeably. Gabe bent down and examined its left front leg, which the animal was favoring. There was an abraded area just above the hock. But that could have come from the fall the horse had taken following the blow.

"Both of us, we're a little worse for the wear," Gabe said in an undertone to the horse as he ran his hands over its shoulders and neck. "But that comes from my bad habit of not learning to mind my own business."

The roan swung its head around to look at him. Was there reproach in its eyes?

Gabe turned his attention to the Comanche, who was still stolidly sitting his saddle and watching him. "You mind my asking why those four fellows had it in for you?"

"I went to visit my brother and his family in a village to the east. On my way home, they came upon me. They chased me." He hesitated. "I fell from my horse." The Indian's eyes dropped, a clear sign of shame at his obviously reluctant admission that he was not a perfect horseman. "They caught and beat me. They said they were going to kill me."

"That's all interesting, but I'm still wondering why the fracas happened in the first place."

"Comanche and Apache make war."

Gabe cocked his head to one side and thoughtfully rubbed his chin, his eyes on the Comanche. "I've heard there's been hot blood between your two tribes of late."

"Comanche kill many Apache."

"What about the Apache? Do they kill many Comanche?"

"Some. They take prisoners. Sell them to Comancheros."

Comancheros.

The word—the name—brought a sour taste to Gabe's mouth. He spat. The Comancheros were a southwestern gang composed mostly of white men, but also numbering among its members were some Mexicans and, on occasion, even an Indian or two, who bartered trade beads and low-grade whiskey with the Indians for cattle and horses they knew had been stolen. The majority of the Comancheros were hardcases who were best avoided, Gabe had learned from experience. Now, he was disgusted to hear, the Comancheros had taken to trading in human merchandise, confirming the rumors he had been hearing as he traveled through the southwest.

"You are hurt."

Gabe looked down at the wound in his left bicep where the blood had begun to dry. "You're right on that score. But it looks like I'll live."

"My name is Sees the Moon and I am a member of the Antelope Band of Comanches."

"Mine's Gabe Conrad. Glad to make your acquaintance."

The Comanche's eyes narrowed. "Gabe Conrad," he repeated. "You are the man the Oglala Sioux call Long Rider?"

Gabe nodded.

"I have heard of you."

"Nothing too bad, I hope," Gabe said with a grin, picking up the bloody knife the dead Apache had used to try to kill him and offering it to Sees the Moon.

"Much good, I have heard," Sees the Moon said, taking the knife and wiping Gabe's blood from it on his buckskin shirt. "Where do you go, Gabe Conrad, who is also Long Rider?"

Gabe shrugged, an answer of sorts.

"You come with me to my village, yes? There is much food there. My people would like to meet the man they have heard spoken of and sung about around their camp fires."

Well, why not, Gabe thought. No one was waiting for him anywhere. There was no place he had to go, or be, at any particular time. Why not, indeed?

"We might as well take along those horses. The Apaches won't have any more need of them," he said as he climbed into the saddle.

Sees the Moon turned his horse and, together with Gabe, rode west, both men herding the Indians' horses ahead of them.

The arrival of Gabe and Sees the Moon in the Comanche village on the eastern bank of the Pecos River caused a commotion that did not surprise Gabe. He knew that the arrival of a white man in an Indian village was bound to create a stir. But the commotion now taking place was due only in part to his presence. People were expressing concern about what had happened to Sees the Moon, who still had dried blood on his face. They wanted to know where the horses that belonged to the Apaches had come from, and when Sees the Moon told them of what had happened there were loud shouts of outrage and calls for revenge from more than one young man.

Then the inevitable question was asked of Sees the Moon.

He answered it by saying, "This is the man the Oglala Sioux call Long Rider." He placed a hand on Gabe's shoulder. "He saved my life."

Silence settled on the camp. Intense black eyes in countless faces stared at Gabe. Then the whispers began. People

told each other that the blond giant was here before them,
and so the legend of Long Rider—it was more than a legend. It was truth. Gabe's presence here among them proved
it.

An old man emerged from the crowd. His braided hair
was white and his face was deeply seamed with the lines
of age. His arms were folded across his chest as he stood
and stared up at Gabe.

"You are welcome to our village," he told Gabe. "Step
down and be with us."

Gabe got out of the saddle.

"I am Chief Ten Bears," the old man told Gabe. "I thank
you for saving the life of Sees the Moon."

"I'm not sure that's exactly how it was, Chief Ten Bears,"
Gabe protested mildly. "It was more like we saved each
other's lives."

"You say," Chief Ten Bears began, addressing Sees the
Moon, "that two of the Apaches escaped alive."

"Yes."

"That is bad news." He glanced at Gabe. "The two you
and Sees the Moon let live, they will go back to their camp
and tell their friends what happened to them. They will want
blood to avenge spilled blood. You are, as I said, welcome
in our camp, Long Rider, but I must warn you that you will
be in danger if you stay with us."

"From those Apaches, you mean? Them and their
friends?"

"It is so," Chief Ten Bears said solemnly.

"If those Apaches take a notion to come looking for me,
they'll not find me hiding from them," Gabe said as solemnly.

"Those are the words of a brave—or a foolish—man,"
Chief Ten Bears observed.

Gabe shrugged.

"Come," said the chief. "In my lodge there is food. You
will eat. Then you will tell us in your own words how you
came to be called Long Rider."

Gabe left Sees the Moon and followed Chief Ten Bears to the center of the village where a lodge was painted with stick figures of Indians and United States cavalrymen doing violent battle. Some of the troopers had lost their scalps. The pictographs gave Gabe a momentary chill. They reminded him, as did so many things, that he was a man with a foot in two worlds, one red, one white. Here he was in the midst of a Comanche camp, and those who lived in the camp, as the pictographs proved, had killed and scalped many white men. The chill passed.

They entered the lodge and Gabe was immediately taken by the dusky beauty of the young woman who was tending a cookfire in the center of the shelter. She looked up shyly as the two men entered the lodge, then turned her attention back to the fire. Using sticks, she placed heated stones in the buffalo paunch that hung from a tripod made of sticks bound with rawhide.

"You did not come to greet our visitor," Chief Ten Bears said to her.

"I saw him," she said. "From just outside the lodge. I thought you might bring him here. So I am cooking."

Chief Ten Bears nodded. "You are a dutiful granddaughter. I am blessed."

The woman, whom Gabe judged to be sixteen or seventeen, said nothing.

"This is Long Rider of the Oglala Sioux," Chief Ten Bears told his granddaughter.

"You are welcome to the village and to our lodge, Long Rider," she said.

"You honor me, you and your grandfather."

"My granddaughter's name is Likes Horses," Chief Ten Bears said. "She is the daughter of my only son, who was killed by the Apaches this year in the Moon of Strawberries. She lost her mother the day she was born. A life came, a life went that day. It is the sometimes sad way of things."

"The food is ready," Likes Horses declared. She filled a bowl with something she took from the buffalo paunch and then filled a slightly larger bowl from a bark cooking pot that sat near the coals at the edge of the fire. She handed them both, together with a buffalo horn spoon, to Gabe, who sat down crosslegged on the dirt floor of the lodge. He began to eat the meal, which turned out to be boiled acorns of the blackjack oak in the smaller bowl and, in the larger bowl, a mush made of buffalo marrow mixed with crushed mesquite beans, which was very sweet because of its high sugar content.

Likes Horses then served her grandfather, after which he asked her to inform the villagers that, when Long Rider had eaten his fill, he would tell his life story to the villagers so that they might learn the truth of the legend from the man who had lived it.

Both men ate in silence after Likes Horses had slipped from the lodge. When they had finished, they set their empty bowls aside and Chief Ten Bears filled the bowl of his pipe with kinnikinnick. After lighting it and blowing smoke in the four directions of the compass, he handed the pipe to Gabe, who did the same.

Later, when the pipe was out, Chief Ten Bears rose and beckoned to Gabe, who followed him outside.

Seated on the ground in the darkness were the villagers. In the distance the surface of the Pecos River glistened in the light of the rising moon. A fire burned between two logs just outside the lodge, adding its light to that of the moon's.

Chief Ten Bears nodded in Gabe's direction. "Speak," he said.

Gabe spoke. "My mother, Amelia, and I were taken captive by the People many years ago when I was but a child. We lived a life we both hated—at first. But in time I came to like the life I was living and to love the People with whom I lived it. So did my mother. She became the wife of a warrior named Little Wound. They were very much in love. . . ."

His eyes settled on Likes Horses, who was seated on

the ground, the firelight illuminating her lovely face, as
he spoke. They remained there as he continued telling the
tale of how Gabe Conrad had become the legendary man
known as Long Rider.

CHAPTER TWO

Gabe awoke the next morning just minutes before the first gray fingers of false dawn crept across the sky. He lay wrapped in his blanket on top of the tarpaulin he had spread next to Chief Ten Bears' lodge and watched a dog wander through the village, snuffling here, poking its nose there, in search of food. He heard the distant song of a meadowlark that might have been welcoming the morning that was about to be. As the gray sky gradually brightened, the lodges stood silhouetted against the sky.

He yawned. Stretched. Watched the first smoky tendrils of a cookfire curl upward from the smokehole of a nearby lodge.

He thought of the night just passed and of how he had told the story of his life in the Oglala camp to the people of this village. He smiled to himself as he thought of how his listeners had *ooohhed* and *aahhed* in wonder and delight, especially when he told of his long ride to warn the Sioux in a distant village of the impending raid by soldiers of the United States. Their cheers, when he had finished his tale, echoed now in his mind and seemed to brighten the morning. His smile broadened as he remembered how the young men had touched him when his tale had been told, as if by doing so they could share with him—what? Luck? Power? The mystique of the man they knew as Long Rider?

His reverie was interrupted when Likes Horses emerged from her grandfather's lodge. As her head began to turn in his direction, Gabe closed his eyes, feigning sleep. When he heard her moving away from the lodge he opened his eyes. Likes Horses was making her way through the village on her way down to the river.

She moved with a kind of natural grace. The sway of her hips, the forward thrust of her shoulders, the way her arms swung and her feet touched the ground with firm purpose— Gabe found her movements arousing. She was, he thought, every inch a woman and then some. Her black hair, bound in braids and decorated with colorful beads, glistened as the sun appeared above the eastern horizon and touched it. The light also made her smooth skin glow.

Gabe threw off his blanket. He shook out his boots and then pulled them on. Rising, he picked up his blanket and tarpaulin and folded them. He placed his bedroll next to the lodge and then headed for the river. On his way to it, he passed the spot where his horse had spent the night with those belonging to the villagers. The young boy of fourteen or so who had spent the night guarding the horses gave him a smile. Then, with a glance at Likes Horses, who was standing on the eastern bank of the river, the boy also gave Gabe a sly wink.

Gabe, thinking that the young grew up far too fast these days, gave him a grin.

Likes Horses heard him coming. She turned and, seeing him, lowered her eyes.

"May this day be good to you," Gabe told her as he knelt on the river bank.

"And to you."

Gabe thrust his hands into the water and proceeded to

wash his face and neck. He rubbed sand on his hands to clean them, aware that Likes Horses had knelt near him and was discreetly performing her own morning ablutions. He did not look directly at her, but he could see her out of the corner of his eye.

When she rose and without a word left the river bank, Gabe did the same. He followed her for some distance until they had left the village far behind them. Likes Horses stopped and picked a small bouquet of wildflowers and then resumed her journey. She stopped at last by a tall shin oak. There she knelt beside the grassy mound at the base of the tree and swept away the remains of some withered flowers that were lying atop what was obviously a grave. Then she placed the flowers she had just picked on the grave—gently, reverently.

Gabe halted and watched her as she knelt there, her body motionless, only her lips moving as she whispered words he could not hear. He was about to turn and leave the spot, intending to leave her alone with her memories and prayers, when she rose and turned.

She showed no surprise at the sight of him. She gestured toward the grave. "My father, Will Not Go, lies there. When he died two moons ago, I thought my heart would break. He was a good man and good to me. He was my father and my mother as well, since she died giving me life. He did not seem to mind that I was a girl and not the son I know he wanted. I miss him still. His passing has left a hole in my heart and I am ashamed."

"I don't understand."

"I want him back. That is a terrible thing to say. He lives now in the land beyond where the sun sets. There the weather is always mild. No snows come. There is no ice to freeze fingers and toes. There is no rain or wind. There the great chiefs of all the Comanches hold their assemblies and there the warriors are all forever young. There is much buffalo, antelope, elk. No one hungers. No one thirsts. There the horses are fleeter than the wind. How dare I wish to take him from that fine world and return him to this imperfect one?"

"You dare," Gabe said, "because you loved—and still love—him."

Likes Horses gazed at him, her eyes uneasy. "But it is wrong for me to want him back, to want to take him from that wonderful world to which he has gone and where he prospers and is happy."

"I believe he would leave it gladly if he could return to you."

Likes Horses bit her lower lip. She turned her head away. She wiped furiously at the tears that sprang to her eyes. Then, surrendering to her grief, she covered her face with her hands and began to sob.

Gabe went to her and took her in his arms. She buried her face, which was still hidden in her hands, against his chest and continued to sob, her shoulders shaking, her tears wetting Gabe's shirt.

She wept for several minutes, then slowly took her hands away from her face and put her arms around Gabe. They stood there then, holding one another, neither of them speaking, Gabe keenly conscious of his growing desire for her, which was being manifested in his stiff and throbbing erection. He shifted position slightly in an effort to keep Likes Horses from becoming aware of his arousal.

"Since my father died, I have no one to love. Oh, my grandfather is good to me and I love him, but that is not the same thing. I want—" Likes Horses suddenly stopped in mid-sentence.

Gabe felt her body stiffen. She stepped back and looked up at him. And then down at the bulge in his jeans.

"I'm sorry. I didn't mean to—I didn't follow you here to—for this. That's the truth. Please believe me."

"I believe you."

"I'll leave."

But, as Gabe turned to go, Likes Horses reached out and gripped his arm.

He halted and looked back at her.

"When I saw you for the first time last evening when you arrived in the village, I felt my heart leap. I wanted you then and I want you now. But not here in this place of loss." She glanced at the grave. "When my father was killed by the Apaches, I felt as if I had died with him. I felt—lifeless. But then last evening you came and I felt desire—felt life—awaken within me once again."

Likes Horses threw herself into Gabe's arms.

He hesitated and then, cupping her chin in his hand, he raised her head and kissed her. At first, she merely accepted his kiss but then, after a moment during which his tongue breached the barrier of her teeth, she responded to his kiss with an ardor that bordered on the ferocious. When their kiss finally ended, both were panting and thoroughly shaken with the strength of their mutual desire.

Likes Horses took Gabe by the hand and led him away from the grave and its burden of bow and quiver. She led him into a shady forest and stopped when she reached a green patch of mossy ground. She lay down upon it, spreading her legs and lifting her skirt.

He knelt between her spread legs and fumbled with the buttons on his jeans. When he had them undone, he shoved his jeans down around his knees and covered her, but he did not immediately enter her. His arms went under and around her, lifting her toward him. His kiss caused her to take his tongue and begin to suck it, but it was his gentle probing of her hot mound that caused her knees to bend and her body to shift position so that he could gain entry easily.

He did. And when he had slowly eased himself all the way into her warm wetness, he withdrew, but not completely, then entered her again and once more began to withdraw.

Her body suddenly lurched beneath him and he found himself all the way within her, his erection pulsing lustily, his hips bucking almost beyond his control. When he exploded inside her a moment later he cursed himself for his haste, for his lack of control, but he continued his plunging as stiff as ever until he felt her body convulse almost violently as a result of her orgasm, and he heard her cry out as her neck arched and she threw her head back.

Shuddering as she was, he slowed his rhythm and gradually became motionless but still stiff within her. He lay on top of her, nuzzling her neck, her earlobes, listening to her rapid breathing and feeling her hands caressing his back, his buttocks, his back again.

He withdrew from her moments later and sat back on her thighs, his shaft stabbing up toward the overhead branches of the tree towering above them.

She reached up and gently stroked his erection. It jerked spasmodically in response. Then she released it and spread her arms out at her sides. A contented sigh escaped her lips.

He pulled up his jeans, buttoned them and flopped down on his back beside her, then leaned over and kissed her lightly on the cheek.

She sighed again. "I wish the killing would stop. So many of our people have died. And they have killed many Apaches. Why is it that men must make war and women weep when their men are slain?"

"I've got no answer for you—at least, none that would make any kind of sense to you. It's just the way the world and the men and women in it are."

"I would change it if I knew how."

"How long have the Comanches and Apaches been at each other's throats?"

"Many moons. The first raid the Apaches made on our village—it was during the Moon of the Hairless Calves. I remember there was snow on the ground. We were camped then to the south of this place. When the battle was over, we moved north, away from the Apache lands. My grandfather said that would stop the raiding. It didn't. Our young men wanted vengeance. So they raided the Apaches. It goes on even now. You know that Sees the Moon was almost killed by the Apaches who caught him. He would have been killed had you not come along to save him from them. But death might be better than being taken prisoner by the Apaches."

"Death is never good."

Likes Horses turned on her side and gazed into Gabe's eyes. "Our people whom the Apache have taken in raids, did you know they sell them to the Comancheros?"

"I'd heard a tale or two to that effect, and Sees the Moon told me about it, yes."

"We do not know what happens to those people, the young men and women they sell. What, we wonder, do the Comancheros do with them? Why do they buy them? For what purpose? We do not know and, not knowing, we are afraid."

"No one has ever escaped and come back to tell what happened to them after they were taken captive by the Apaches and sold to the Comancheros?"

Likes Horses shook her head. "No one has ever returned. I am not sure I want to know what has happened to them because the Comancheros are evil men. Some of our people have traded with them. They have traded horses to them for bad whiskey and beads and the like, although my grandfather has forbidden them to do so."

Likes Horses seemed to shudder. She wrapped her arms about herself as if to ward off a chill and rose. "We must go back. I must cook. It is time to eat and begin the day."

As they neared the camp, Gabe heard the sounds of women's laughter and the shouts of men. When they arrived in the camp, he found it bustling with activity. Women were packing buffalo skins on the backs of horses. Men were sharpening their lances and their arrows.

"What's going on?" he asked Likes Horses. "Are you breaking camp today?"

Likes Horses shook her head. "We go to hunt buffalo today."

As they approached Ten Bears' lodge, Sees the Moon came running up to them.

"Long Rider, you will go with us to hunt the buffalo?"

The question sparked a rush of memories in Gabe's mind of all the other buffalo hunts he had been on. Excitement surged within him. Although he had been thinking vaguely of leaving the Comanche camp that day, the prospect of a buffalo hunt made him decide to remain. Or was it the prospect of the impending hunt that kept him where he was? He glanced at the woman by his side. No, he realized, it was not just the hunt that made him want to linger with the Comanches. It was something more. And that something more went by the name of Likes Horses.

"Will you hunt with us, Long Rider?" Sees the Moon was asking.

"I will," Gabe said, causing a smile to brighten the faces of both Sees the Moon and Likes Horses.

"We make ready to leave for our temporary hunting camp," Sees the Moon declared. "The scouts we sent to search for the buffalo returned this morning. They say there is a large herd grazing to the southwest. We go there now."

"We have not yet had breakfast," Likes Horses said. "We will eat and then we will go."

As Sees the Moon loped off to his own lodge, Likes Horses left Gabe and began to prepare the morning meal. As she was doing so, Ten Bears came out of his lodge.

"Are you going on the hunt?" Gabe asked the chief.

"No, I do not go anymore to hunt. These bones of mine, they grow old and do not always do as I would wish. I leave the hunting now to the young men. Will you go, Long Rider?"

"Yes, I will go. It has been a long time since I hunted the buffalo. I am looking forward to doing so once again."

"But this time, for you, it will be different."

"How so?" a puzzled Gabe inquired.

Ten Bears pointed to Gabe's gear, which was piled beside the lodge. "Now you will hunt with the gun you have there." He indicated the Winchester. "When you were with the

Oglala, you did not hunt with a gun, is that not so?"

"That is so."

Ten Bears nodded. "Times change. Sometimes for the better. Sometimes not."

Later, as the three ate the meal Likes Horses had prepared, Gabe pondered the old chief's words. It was true, he thought, as he raked a roasted turtle from the fire and cracked its shell with a stone. Times do change. Sometimes they change so fast it's enough to make a man's head swim. They changed for Gabe when he left the People and went out into the white world, and he wasn't sure he'd yet recovered from that experience. He scooped meat out of the shell of the turtle with his fingers and ate it.

Likes Horses kicked back into the fire a turtle that had tried to escape from it. From the other side of the fire, she gave Gabe a secret smile.

When Gabe had finished feasting on his share of the roasted turtles, Likes Horses served him grapes, some of which he dutifully took and ate, though his stomach was already filled almost to the bursting point.

After all three had finished eating and had washed their hands and rinsed their mouths with water that Likes Horses had served in small bark bowls, they went outside to find many of the young men and women already leaving the camp.

Gabe frowned and asked, "Why is it that some of the young men are going to the southeast? Sees the Moon told me the herd had been sighted in the southwest."

"Those men who are riding to the southeast," Ten Bears answered, "they do not go to hunt buffalo. They go instead to hunt Apaches."

"Are you coming with us on the hunt?" Gabe asked Likes Horses.

"Yes. I will help with the work when the hunt is over," she replied.

They bade good-bye to Ten Bears, who wished them a successful hunt and, after Gabe had picked up his gear, they

headed for the corral, where Gabe retrieved his roan and
Likes Horses took possession of a dappled mare. She waited
while Gabe saddled and bridled his horse and placed his rifle
in its saddle scabbard. Then they rode out together, following the procession of men and women heading southwest.

They traveled at a steady pace for many miles and did
not stop to make a nooning when the sun reached its meridian. Instead they traveled on, the men occasionally raising
their voices in song and sometimes telling tall tales about
their experiences during previous hunts, tales which were a
harmless mixture of pure fancy and outright lies. But they
became quiet the closer they came to their destination.

In mid-afternoon the scout at the head of the hunting party held up a hand and the group halted. He pointed to the
spot he had selected for their temporary hunting camp, a
place where a stream flowed and there was a good supply
of timber.

Then the work began. Packhorses were relieved of their
burdens. Tents were constructed using the skins the horses
had been carrying, which were thrown over poles that rested
on crossed stakes. Gabe helped construct a scaffold to be
used later for drying the meat of the slain buffalo.

When all the tents were up and the scaffold was finished
and each hunter was in possession of his weapons, the men
gathered in a circle to select the one who would be their
hunt leader.

Gabe was talking to Like Horses near the scaffold when
Sees the Moon stepped out of the group of consulting men,
pointed a finger at Gabe and called out, "Hunt leader."

Gabe was taken aback. He had not considered the possibility of himself being elected to lead the hunt. He had not
even taken part in the discussion of who the leader should
be, since he did not know the men involved and thus was
in no position to judge which of them had the requisite qualities—good judgment, fearlessness, strong hunting skills—
to be designated the leader of the hunt.

He could not refuse to lead the men. To do so would be

to insult them. They had chosen him on the basis of what they knew about him, and the fact that he was chosen was, he knew, an unmistakable tribute and honor.

"You will lead us, Long Rider?" Sees the Moon called out.

"I will."

A cheer went up from the group of hunters.

"You," Gabe said, pointing to a young man in the crowd. "You will go and find the herd and then return to tell us where it is."

The young man, a broad smile on his face, ran from the group of hunters, leaped aboard a barebacked buckskin and went galloping out of the camp.

While he was gone, Gabe discussed tactics with the other hunters. They agreed to ride up on the herd in a large semicircle and then, as they came closer to it, spread out until they had surrounded it.

"Before we attack, we've got to make sure we move up on them against the wind," Gabe said. "You men all know that the buffalo have a sharp sense of smell, so we don't want to let them know we're coming."

Gabe listened to the suggestions made by a number of the men. He agreed with many of them, rejected others. He concluded the discussion by saying, "Let's get one thing straight. I don't want any of you jumping the gun. We'll all charge at once. If we don't do it that way, we run the risk of scattering the herd. Also, we want to kill as many buffalo as we can as fast as we can."

A boy Gabe judged to be no more than fourteen asked, "Why do we have to kill them as fast as we can?"

Some of his elders smiled to themselves as Gabe said, "I take it this is your first hunt."

"My second," the youngster answered proudly.

"Maybe nobody's ever told you this before, but the reason we want to make fast kills is because the buffalo's meat will spoil long before the women can cure it if the animals are killed after they've been run ragged for a long time and their bodies are all overheated."

"I didn't know that," the boy said sheepishly.

"A man lives and learns," Gabe told him, and didn't miss the way pride flared in the youngster's eyes as a result of the implication of Gabe's remark—that he was not a boy but a man.

The scout returned half an hour later to lead the hunters to their quarry.

Gabe was about to step into his saddle when his eyes fell on the stock of his rifle. His gaze shifted to the other men, who were all carrying bows or lances as they climbed aboard the bare backs of their horses. When in Rome . . . , he thought to himself. He removed his saddle from the roan, along with the Winchester. He unbuckled his cartridge belt and left it and the gun that hung from it with the rest of his gear in the care of Likes Horses. From her he obtained a length of rawhide, and this he looped around the lower jaw of his roan to use as a bridle as the Comanches were doing. He asked Sees the Moon if he could borrow the man's lance and it was given to him gladly. He was not unaware of the fact that the Indians were giving him approving glances as he went about adopting their hunting customs. To use his rifle to make a kill, he had realized, would give him an unfair advantage over the other men. But there was another reason for not bringing his gun and for choosing to ride the way the Indians were riding: By doing so, he was able to relive the way he had lived while hunting buffalo as a boy among the Oglala. It was, he thought, a little like coming home after a long absence. He raised his hand and gave the signal to move out.

The scout rode ahead of Gabe. With Gabe rode the men. Behind them came the women on the horses that would, if the hunt were successful, become packhorses loaded with meat and hides to bring back to the camp.

They rode in silence, walking their horses to avoid making any unnecessary noise that might alert the animals to their approach and cause them to flee.

Gabe, as he rode, felt the familiar excitement of the hunt rising within him. It had always been this way. When he had ridden with the People to hunt buffalo, there had always been this sense of excitement. It was always coupled with a faint sense of unease for, if the hunt failed or if the take was small, the days to come would be hungry ones.

When the scout slowed his mount and held up a hand, Gabe and the others also slowed their horses. They rounded a bend and there were the buffalo! But there also were a number of hills across which the buffalo ranged. They dotted the sides of the hills and grazed idly in the shallow valleys between them.

Gabe beckoned to the other hunters. When they had ridden up to him, he said, "We're not going to be able to make a surround, not in this terrain, we're not. What we'll do is line up side by side and, when I give the signal, we'll make a head-on charge. The men on the flanks of the line should try to run into a pack once we get beyond those hills and out onto the open prairie again. If you can do that, then we can make a surround in the usual way and complete our kill. Everybody get that?"

Heads nodded. There were murmurs of assent. Then all the men formed a straight line with Gabe at its center. He waited until everyone was in place and then gave the signal to charge. The men slammed their heels into their horses and went racing forward toward the great beasts, whose hides were in prime condition since the moulting season had ended.

Suddenly, as the line broke and the men went after their individually chosen targets, the twang of bowstrings filled the air. Gabe saw one of the beasts go down on his left while the others lifted their horned heads in alarm and then, as the hunters closed in on them, began to run. He chose the animal he intended to go after—a large bull with a ragged scar on its right flank that bore clear testimony that the animal had been hunted before but had survived.

Gripping the rawhide bridle in his right hand, Gabe raised

the lance in his left hand as he galloped toward his quarry. He came up on the buffalo from the rear as it raced away from him and began to close in on the bull's right side. The animal, either sensing or actually seeing his presence, suddenly veered sharply to the left turned in a tight circle, and raced back the way it had come. Gabe, taken by surprise by the maneuver, rode on for a few yards before he was able to slow his horse's forward momentum and turn it to resume pursuit of his prey.

He quickly caught up with the racing bull and this time, alert for any sudden moves it might make, he gradually managed to close the distance that separated them from one another. As he came closer to the animal, he almost choked as a result of the thick cloud of dust it had stirred up in its headlong flight and which had invaded his nostrils and throat. Swallowing hard to clear his throat and blowing as hard to clear his nostrils, he raced on after the buffalo. He raised the lance in his hand, took careful aim, and the instant he was close enough threw the lance in a downward and forward trajectory from his position directly behind and above the buffalo.

He let out a loud whoop of triumph as his lance struck the exact spot he had aimed at—the soft spot between the protruding hip bone and the animal's last rib, where he knew its heart hung low in its body. His lance, thrown with immense force, had passed all the way through the animal, its spearhead protruding from the opposite side of its body.

As the animal dropped heavily to the ground in death, Gabe veered away from his kill and rode out to the left flank of the line of hunters, to help the men there drive the animals onto the plain where they could be more readily surrounded and thus more easily killed. He joined two men who were howling at the tops of their voices and waving their lances and bows in the air to frighten the buffalo. As the animals raced away from them, they joined other buffalo who were being hazed from the opposite flank by other hunters. Soon the animals were surrounded on three sides by armed men.

As they all emerged from the hilly region onto the open plain, Gabe and the other flankers rode forward and then cut directly in front of the buffalo to complete the surround. The running bulls instinctively sought to protect the cows and calves by driving them into the middle of the herd. When they had succeeded in doing so, the bulls proceeded to race around and around the pack in circles, presenting themselves broadside to the hunters and thereby unwittingly making of themselves easy targets. One after another of the bulls went down with arrows or lances in their bodies. Then two of the bulls, apparently confused and bewildered, simply stopped in their tracks and ran no more.

Sees the Moon, with a *yip-yip-yipay*, brought one of the pair down with an arrow. Another hunter killed the second bull with a lance. Soon the cows and calves were vulnerable. A few cows were killed but no calves. The hunters left the latter to grow up and provide targets for another day, perhaps for the last months of the present year when they would be older and meatier and their hides would be covered with a dark, seal-brown fur that would make excellent winter robes.

When the killing was finally over, the hunters spread out to claim their individual kills. Dead buffalo were identified by the hunters as their own when they recognized their arrows in the animals or by the location of the corpses. Sometimes a hunter was able to recognize his kill by the location of the wounds he had made in the animal's body. As the identification process went on a dispute broke out between two of the hunters, each of whom had left arrows in a dead buffalo and each of whom now claimed the kill as his own. As was the custom in such cases, Gabe, as leader of the hunt, was called upon to settle the dispute.

He examined the dead buffalo and the positions of the arrows. "This arrow," he said, pointing to one of the two in the body of the buffalo, "entered the kidneys. It would have crippled the animal and slowed it down, if not stopped it entirely."

The hunter whose arrow Gabe was speaking of began to smile.

But then Gabe pointed to the other man's arrow and said, "This is the one that killed the buffalo. It is plain to see that it has entered the heart. In my judgment, the kill properly belongs to the man whose arrow pierced the heart of this buffalo."

The man who had been smiling now wore a glum expression.

"But I would suggest," Gabe continued, "that the kill be divided equally between the two hunters whose arrows are in this buffalo. It can be argued that the kidney strike that crippled and probably slowed the animal gave the man who struck at the heart his chance. What say you, men?"

The two hunters stared at each other for a moment, then at the buffalo, then at Gabe.

"Well?" he prompted.

The man to whom the kill rightfully belonged, as decided by Gabe, nodded. Then he clapped the other hunter on the back and together they began to butcher their kill.

Gabe drew his knife and made his way over to where the buffalo he had downed was lying. All around him men were busy butchering dead buffalo. Unlike the Sioux, whose women did the butchering following a hunt, the Comanche men were the ones who performed this task.

He passed cows that had been left lying on their sides, and when he reached his kill, he heaved the dead bull over onto its belly with all four of its legs spread. He slashed the neck of the animal and then folded back the flesh so that he could remove the forequarters at the joint. Then he sliced down the middle of the spine to cut the sinews, which he proceeded to remove intact.

Later, after he had peeled the hide back on both sides, he disjointed the hindquarters, leaving the rump with the back of the animal. Unmindful of the blood that stained his hands and had spattered in places on his clothes, he cut into the flank and removed it together with the brisket. The chunk that resulted was made up of one roll of meat.

Sees the Moon, who was busily butchering a cow some distance away, called out to Gabe and beckoned. Leaving his partially carved up bull behind, Gabe made his way over to where Sees the Moon was kneeling on the ground beside his kill.

"A treat, Long Rider," Sees the Moon said, a knife in one hand and his free hand resting on the cow's udder. "You want some?"

Gabe realized what he was being offered and realized too that it was a long time since he had tasted—

Sees the Moon made a cut in the cow's udder and then looked up at Gabe.

Gabe knelt down beside the man and bent over to place his mouth on the cut. He sucked the warm mixture of milk and blood from the slashed udder with remembered pleasure, and then raised his head and let Sees the Moon take his place.

"I'm obliged to you," he said. "It's been a while since I tasted that kind of treat."

"More?"

Gabe shook his head. "You go ahead and finish it off. I'll get back to my butchering." He made his way back the way he had come, passing men and women who were hungrily devouring raw buffalo kidneys and tallow. One man had removed the entrails from the bull he had killed and was engaged in removing their contents by running them through his fingers and then devouring them.

When he got back to his bull, he found Likes Horses there waiting for him.

"I see your hunting was successful," she remarked as he hunkered down and cut up through the ventral to remove the entrails and separate the ribs from the sternum.

"This meat—it's yours and your grandfather's," he told her.

"You are kind. It is hard for grandfather and me now that he is too old to hunt and there is no other man in our lodge. But other hunters share their kills with us."

"If it's all right with you, I'd like to keep a little of this meat to turn into jerky for the trail," Gabe said as he broke the buffalo ribs with his bare hands to free the rib steaks from the spine.

"It is your kill. Take what you need." Likes Horses hesitated a moment and then said, "You say you need meat for the trail. You will leave us now?"

Gabe, his face flecked with buffalo blood, looked up at her. "I'll be moving on, yes."

Likes Horses lowered her eyes. Then she turned and left without another word. When she returned, she was carrying several skins.

Gabe, having finished his butchering, helped her pack the skins full of meat and bind them with rawhide thongs. Together they carried the skins to Likes Horses' dapple, on which they packed the meat.

Likes Horses said nothing as she began to lead her horse back to the hunting camp. Gabe, when she had gone, retrieved Sees the Moon's lance, went to his horse and rode away from the killing field.

By the time he reached the temporary camp, it was alive with activity. Returned hunters, their work done, were feasting on roasted buffalo meat and telling of their exploits during the hunt. Women were slicing buffalo meat into thin fillets, which they hung on the scaffold to dry in the sun. Other women were pegging hides to the ground, flesh side up, so that they could be scraped for later tanning.

Riding over to the gathered group of hunters, Gabe returned the lance he had borrowed from Sees the Moon.

"We did well," Sees the Moon declared happily. "Thanks to you."

"No thanks to me," Gabe said. "We did good because you fellows are hell on the hoof when it comes to hunting. I had all I could do to hold my own among you."

Laughter rose from the men listening to him.

Gabe gave them a wave, then rode over to the stream and along its bank until he reached a spot about a mile from the camp, where he found what he had been seeking—some privacy. He stripped and plunged into the cool water that bounced and gurgled its way around partially submerged rocks. He vigorously scrubbed his body with sand from the streambed and soon no traces of buffalo blood remained on him anywhere. He climbed out of the water and proceeded to wash his clothes, scrubbing them on a rock, rinsing them and then scrubbing them once more to rid them of blood as well.

When he was satisfied that they were as clean as he could get them, he spread them out on the grass to dry. Then, lying down on his back near them, he closed his eyes and folded his hands behind his head, letting the sun dry him as well as his clothes.

She didn't like it, he thought. Likes Horses didn't like it one little bit when he told her he was planning on hitting the trail. In truth, Gabe didn't much like the idea either. Well, there was no hurry to leave, he reminded himself. So he wouldn't—not yet.

He reached out and felt his clothes. Still wet. He became impatient for them to dry so that he could return to the camp and see Likes Horses again. In the end, his impatience won out. He put his clothes on while they were still damp and rode back to the camp.

CHAPTER THREE

On the morning of the hunting party's return to the Comanche camp on the bank of the Pecos River, a scout arrived in the village to announce the successful outcome of the raid the warriors had made on the Apaches.

The population of the village, already joyous over the success of their buffalo hunt, became even more jubilant at the news. Work was forgotten as the people set about making preparations to celebrate the victory. Food was prepared. War bonnets were preened and made ready for wearing. Singers and drummers gathered for their roles in the celebration. When all was ready for the triumphal entry into camp of those who had fought the Apaches, both men and women dressed appropriately for the special occasion and painted their faces—black for the women, red for the men. Those men entitled to wear war bonnets donned them.

Gabe stood with Chief Ten Bears and Likes Horses near the spot where wood had been placed in a conical pile with dry grass beneath it so that it could, at the appropriate moment, be readily set ablaze.

When the first of the returning warriors came into view in the distance, a shout went up from the assembled people at the sight of an Apache scalp being carried on the trip of an upright lance. As the procession of young men came closer, more scalps became visible on their lances and tomahawks. Gabe was easily able to identify the warrior who had been the most brave during the battle by the fact that, as was the Comanche custom in such cases, he was entitled to tie the scalp he had taken to the lower lip of his horse to show his disdain for the enemy he had just successfully fought.

Gabe, together with the others in the village, went to meet the returning men. People shouted and yelled in their excitement. The women broke into a song of praise for their heros.

"We have had our revenge upon our enemy," Chief Ten Bears declared as he walked along beside Gabe. "It tastes sweet."

He halted when he reached the first of the war party, which was being led by the young man who had tied the scalp he had taken to his horse's lip. Holding up his hands, the chief intoned a blessing on the warriors and then praised them for their bravery and congratulated them on the success of their dangerous venture.

"You have shown the Apache that we are not dogs to be kicked nor weaklings to be tormented at will. You have shown them that we are men of courage and skill at making war upon those who would enslave and kill us. We honor you."

Chief Ten Bears turned then and amid more singing, shouting and general merrymaking, led the way back to the village, the warriors holding high the scalps they had taken.

Many of the warriors, as they came to their own lodges, dismounted and turned their horses over to a wife, a mother or a sister, then went inside to rest and prepare for the Scalp Dance that would take place that evening. Some, however, began immediately to feast on the many foods the women had prepared in their honor.

Gabe watched one of the young men as he took up a position in front of his lodge and began to dress the scalp that he had removed from the end of his tomahawk. He carefully scraped the flesh from the skin, he then took a willow twig and bent it into a hoop somewhat larger than the scalp, and secured the twig's ends with a piece of sinew. He then proceeded to sew the outer edges of the scalp he had cleaned to the hoop, pulling the threads of sinew taut in order to stretch the scalp.

Gabe noted that he conscientiously followed the proper procedure for such sewing, which was from east to south, to west, to north, to east—the same direction in which a Comanche entered a lodge. Then he carefully combed and diligently oiled the hair. When he was satisfied with his efforts, he rose and fastened his trophy to the tall slender scalp pole that was embedded in the ground outside his lodge so that it might dry.

Gabe watched for a moment as the Comanche stared up at his prize and the black Apache scalp lock stirred in the wind. Then he turned and walked away.

That night, as Gabe stood with Likes Horses and Chief Ten Bears in the center of the village, the pile of wood and dry grass was ignited and quickly began to brighten the area. Gabe glanced up at the large pole that had been raised not far from the bonfire. From it dangled the Apache scalps that the Comanche warriors had taken. They moved eerily in the wind that was blowing, as if possessed of a ghostly life of their own.

Drums began to sound, their thudding music loud and arousing. Men and women began to dance, their feet pounding the hard ground, their bodies bending forward and then backward again as they faced each other in a long line. The light of the blazing fire made their eyes glow and the sweat that soon formed on their faces seem to flicker, as if they were grimacing or, perhaps, grinning devilishly.

The sound of the drums blended with the pounding of the

dancers' feet, and to Gabe the sound was almost hypnotic. He watched without speaking as the dancers' long line broke and re-formed into a large circle, which then moved about the tall scalp pole and the drummers seated crosslegged at its base.

They began to sing, their voices low, as they continued to circle the scalp pole. They sang of victory and of counting coup. They sang of the bravery of Comanche warriors and of their pride as a people.

"What's he doing?" Gabe asked Likes Horses as Sees the Moon broke through the circle of dancers and took up a position with his back against the scalp pole and his hands reaching behind him to grip it.

It was Ten Bears who answered the question. "Sees the Moon pretends to be an Apache prisoner. Watch."

Gabe watched as several dancers, all of them women, broke from the circle, which closed behind them, and approached the "prisoner" who was pantomiming being bound to the scalp pole. One of the women stopped and withdrew a burning brand from the fire. Her action caused a fiery shower of sparks to shoot up toward the sky. She brandished the flaming stick in her hand and then, still dancing and still singing, jabbed it at Sees the Moon as if she were burning him with it, although her brand never actually touched his body. But he, playing the part of a bound captive, threw back his head and howled as if he had truly been burned. The woman who was pretending to torture "the captive" squealed in delight. She turned to face the dancers circling behind her and raised her brand high above her head. They cheered her.

She gave way to another woman in whose hand a knife had suddenly appeared. The woman with the knife danced around the scalp pole and Sees the Moon, slashing at him with her knife—at his face, at his body, and finally at his groin.

Despite himself and despite his knowledge that the whole performance was a pantomime of the actual act of torturing an Apache prisoner, Gabe winced. The performance was too realistic for his taste.

Sees the Moon screamed.

The woman wiped her knife on her buckskin dress as if to cleanse it of his blood.

The dancers were singing more loudly now, but their song was occasionally interrupted by a collective cheer as the women inside the circle continued to torture their Apache prisoner.

Some time later, the torture act ended and Sees the Moon, an actor to the end, slumped against the scalp pole as he pretended to be dead. But then, as the women withdrew and the circle broke up, men and women danced individually.

Into their midst leaped a man carrying a whip. Its handle was a wood blade with a serrated edge, upon which were carved scalp symbols, and from its end hung two short otter-skin lashes. He raised his whip, and the dancers stopped dancing and listened to him as he recited the story of a coup he had counted. When he finished his recital, he uttered a loud sun curse upon himself as testimony to the truth of what he had just recounted.

"Will you dance?" Likes Horses asked Gabe.

Before he could answer her question, the holder of the whip came up to him and pointed his whip at him.

"What is this?" Gabe asked as the whip-holder raised his whip as if to strike him.

"The holder of the whip has the right to order any spectator to dance," Chief Ten Bears explained to Gabe. "If the spectator refuses, he can be whipped."

Likes Horses settled the matter by taking Gabe by the hand and leading him out among the dancers.

As she began to dance, so did Gabe. The drums urged him on. The singing of the people keened in his ears. He lifted and lowered his feet, stamping the earth as if he would pound it to pieces. In front of him Likes Horses danced, her black hair flying about her face, her eyes aglow and fixed on his face. He matched her movements, watching her watch him. Something powerful passed between them. He felt it. It was more than mere attraction and stronger than sexual desire. It was a kind of unspoken communion that brought warmth to his heart and balm to his body. He basked in the sensations that had no name he knew of.

Maybe it's the dancing, he thought. Or the drums. He danced on, his body moving rhythmically in front of Likes Horses, who was moving closer and closer to him. He felt a sense of heat and knew without knowing how he knew that it was not a result of his physical exertions and that it did not come from the bonfire. He reached out to take Likes Horses' hand but she withdrew from him. Above the din being made by the singers and the dancers and the pounding drums, he heard the words she spoke—or rather, read her lips as she spoke them.

"Don't go."

"I—" He never got to finish what he was about to say. A man danced between him and Likes Horses, cutting off his view of her and silencing him.

The man was wearing a buffalo-scalp bonnet decorated with a neat row of eagle feathers. The breast feathers were tied about the bottom of the quills and reached down to his waist. At the top of the buffalo scalp was a bunch of magpie feathers set back on the center of the head.

The man grunted audibly and continuously and his hands, which were formed into fists, rose and fell as he danced. His eyes were afire with enthusiasm for what he was doing. He was looking directly at Gabe, who had the eerie feeling that the man was not actually seeing him. He moved around the man in order to rejoin Likes Horses.

She was gone. He could see her nowhere. He moved in and out among the dancers circling the scalp pole in search of her, but she was nowhere to be found. He left the dance and went over to where Ten Bears was standing and watching the festivities.

"I seem to have lost your granddaughter," he told the chief.

"She left the dance. She has gone with some of the other women to prepare the feast. It will be served soon." Ten Bears suddenly began to laugh.

Gabe glanced in the direction the chief was looking and saw what was causing the man's laughter. A warrior was dancing—but backward. Every move he made was an inversion of the normal dance steps. When the dancers turned to the right, he turned to the left. If they danced forward, he danced backward. He wore a long sash over his shoulder and carried a buffalo-scrotum rattle that he shook as he danced.

"He is a *pukutsi*," Ten Bears told Gabe. "A crazy warrior."

Ten Bears' brief statement explained the matter, and the man, to Gabe. Many of the Plains Indian tribes, he knew, had such warriors who were the bravest of the brave and who always did everything backward. Such men could be found among the Cheyennes, who called them "Contrary Ones," and among the Crows, who called them "Crazy Dogs Wishing to Die." Such a man, when in battle, would take the free end of the sash he wore over his shoulder and fasten it to the ground with an arrow, there to take his stand during the fight. With bow in one hand and rattle in the other, he stood singing, tethered by his sash. He neither fought nor charged but sang his songs until victory was won or death came to claim him. Only a friend could come and free him. Should he at any time during the battle give way or release himself, the other warriors would taunt him after the fighting was finished in an attempt to goad him into committing an overt act against them, so that they could then in good conscience kill him.

Gabe, as he watched the *pukutsi*, noticed that the other dancers gave him a wide berth. Such a man, he mused, has the aura of a saint. Or a demon. In any case, he is not a run-of-the-mill man, but rather someone special in a faintly frightening way. No wonder the other dancers avoided close contact with him.

A cheer went up from the spectators in response to the approach of numerous women, all of them bearing food that would constitute the feast planned to celebrate not only the Comanches' victory over their enemies, the Apache, but also the successful buffalo hunt recently concluded.

With the appearance of the serving women, Likes Horses among them, the dance came to an abrupt end. The dancers and spectators alike seated themselves on the ground around the serving dishes and eagerly began to devour the food heaped high on the bark bowls and platters.

Gabe helped himself to a chunk of roasted buffalo hump that he smeared with a sauce made from honey, water and buffalo tallow. Ten Bears, who was seated beside him, sampled the boiled buffalo tongue that was garnished with kiln-dried corn that had been boiled and then mashed into a thick paste.

The feasting Comanches passed bowls and plates back and forth among themselves. Gabe passed up the sun-dried hackberries, which had been pulped, mixed with fat, and roasted in the form of small balls. He washed down the remains of the buffalo hump with a drink of boiled cornmeal that had been sweetened with mesquite, thinking that if the Comanches had let the cornmeal concoction ferment, as did the Gila River tribes in Arizona Territory, they would have had themselves a powerful alcoholic mead instead of the tame drink he was presently enjoying. Just as well, he decided. Had the Comanches fermented the cornmeal, the celebration might well have degenerated into a drunken orgy.

"My granddaughter tells me you are planning to leave us," Ten Bears commented as he scooped up in his fingers some of the cornmeal mash and placed it in his mouth.

"I told her that, yes."

"Where do you go, Long Rider?"

"No place in particular."

Ten Bears accepted, from the man on his right, a bark bowl full of pecan nuts. He took a handful and began to pop them into his mouth, one by one. "You are welcome to stay with us as long as you like."

"I know that and I appreciate your offer of hospitality. But the fact is, I'm just not the kind of man that can stay very long in one place. I've got to be on the move. I guess I just can't stand not knowing what's over the hill and around the bend in the crick."

Ten Bears nodded. "You have the wandering feet of the young. They go where the wind takes them. When they grow old, then it is time to sit in the warm sun and remember the days gone by."

Gabe said nothing as he watched Likes Horses make her way through the feasting people toward him. He shifted position to make room for her by his side. When she reached him, she looked at the empty bowl in front of him and then at the one in front of her grandfather. "The food, I take it, was good."

"Tasty," Gabe said as she sat down beside him and her grandfather belched his approval of the meal. "Did you have a chance to get something to eat for yourself or were you too busy feeding all the rest of us?"

"I had some plums and persimmon cakes."

"I go now," Ten Bears said, rising and stretching. "When I was a young man I could dance and sing from sunset to sunrise and be ready to make war in the morning. But now I grow weary and all I do is watch others dance and make merry. Make the most of things while you are young, you two. Too soon the time for pleasure and carousing ends. Too soon," he repeated and sadly shook his head before wandering away in the direction of his lodge.

"About what you said to me during the dance," Gabe began.

"I know there is nothing I can say that will make you stay with us," Likes Horses said softly.

"I've enjoyed being here with you. It's just that I seem to get itchy when I've been in the same place for any length of time. I've just got to get up and get a move on."

"Do you know when you will leave us?"

"No. Not for sure. Soon though. Tomorrow, maybe."

Likes Horses looked away. "So soon?"

Gabe was silent.

"I suppose I should not feel sad. I had a chance to be with you in the little time you were here. That was a good thing which I shall long remember."

"Speaking of that"—Gabe eased closer to Likes Horses—"I was thinking that maybe you and me, we could sort of sneak off somewhere—maybe to the place we went before, and, well, you know."

"Now?"

"Why not?"

Likes Horses looked around at the people surrounding them. "You wait here. I will go first. Then you follow me."

Gabe agreed to the plan, aware that Likes Horses did not want the world, in the form of her friends and neighbors, to know her personal business. He sat where he was and watched her thread her way through the crowd as she headed for the river. He suppressed the strong urge to leap up and run after her. He absently accepted a persimmon cake that someone offered him and began to eat it. He ordered himself to count to one hundred. But he never made it to his goal. When he reached fifty, he got to his feet . . .

And froze at the sound of the blood-curdling war whoop that suddenly burst out of the darkness from an unseen throat.

For one alarmed instant, there was sudden and absolute silence in the Comanche camp. Then screams rent it. So did roars of rage from the young men. People leaped to their feet, spilling bowls and baskets of food and overturning platters. Women fled, some with children. The men ran to their lodges and emerged with weapons to find the camp completely overrun with armed Apaches, some on horseback, most on foot. The marauders' continuing war whoops now blended with those of the Comanche men who began to do savage battle with them.

Gabe had run to Ten Bears' lodge even before the sound

of the first Apache war whoop had faded away and now, as
men battled one another at close quarters in hand-to-hand
fashion, he stood with his feet firmly planted apart. With
both hands gripping his Colt, he fired a shot that lifted an
Apache, who was racing toward him with a war club raised
above his head, off his feet and threw him backward to
collide with Ten Bears, who had been pursuing him.

Ten Bears was knocked to the ground and the knife he had
had in his hand went skidding across the ground. He turned
and scrabbled along the ground in an effort to retrieve it, but
he never did because a moccasined Apache foot descended
on the wrist of his desperately reaching right hand and
pinned it to the ground. At the same moment, the Apache
raised the lance in his hand, ready to plunge it into Ten
Bears' body and thus pin it to the ground as he had just
pinned the chief's hand.

But, before the lance could make its deadly descent, Gabe
squeezed off a second shot. This one plowed into the side of
the Apache's neck and ripped it wide open as it exited from
the man's flesh. The Apache let go of his lance, staggered,
and then reached up with both hands as if to right his head,
which had tilted to one side as a result of the damage done
by Gabe's strategically aimed round. The man took a step.
Another. He fell.

And was immediately replaced by another warrior, who
had seen what had just happened and, ignoring Ten Bears
as he got to his feet, threw the knife in his hand at Gabe.

The knife ripped into and through the hide covering of
Ten Bears' lodge instead of its intended target because,
Gabe, even before the knife had left the Apache's hand,
had ducked so that it went harmlessly over his head.

The Apache screamed in frustration, the sound blending
with the screams of Comanche women and the wailing of
their frightened children.

Gabe, firing as he went, ran to Ten Bears and almost lifted
the man bodily, one of his shots downing the knife-throwing
Apache who had just tried to kill him. Everywhere people

were fighting. Or fleeing. Smoke filled the camp now from the burning lodges the Apaches had torched. Gabe, with an arm firmly around Ten Bears' waist, hurried the old man out of the camp and over to the relative safety of some chokecherry bushes that grew some distance away.

"Stay here," he told the old man. "Don't expose your position. Those Apaches outnumber us, I'd guess, by at least two to one. I'll be back."

Gabe, as he raced back to where the battle was still being waged, thumbed cartridges from his belt and filled the empty chambers of his .44. He peered through the choking smoke in search of Likes Horses but saw her nowhere. He could, however, see the bodies that littered the ground among the lodges, both Comanche and Apache. A few were not dead, and one of those few screamed in agony as he frantically clutched at the bloody stump of his left arm—the stump from which, apparently, a tomahawk had severed his hand.

Gabe dodged a bright burst of fire that shot out from a lodge as it burned. The heat it gave off, together with the other fires that were burning in the camp, wrung sweat from his face and body, which almost immediately became sooty as the smoke blended with it. Before long Gabe's face was almost black because of this and it looked as if he, like the Apaches, had painted himself for war.

A Comanche woman raced past him, her hair flying out behind her. Gabe recognized her as one of the serving women. She was being pursued by a mounted Apache who was war whooping loudly and grinning evilly. Gabe had to shoot him twice before he died and fell from his horse. But the man had thrown the war club in his hand before Gabe's first round bit into his body. Gabe turned and was sickened at the sight of the Comanche woman's brains, which were splattered on the ground all around her fallen body because of the war club, which had savagely struck her on the back of the head, shattering her skull.

He wiped his eyes free of sweat and ran through the camp

past the bodies of men, women and children, which bristled with arrows like some grotesque species of porcupine. He shouted Likes Horses' name but received no answer.

When he turned and began to retrace his steps, he became aware that something had changed. The dense smoke prevented him at first from seeing what that something was. But, as a wayward breeze blew through the camp, momentarily clearing the area around him of smoke from the burning lodges, he knew what was different. There were fewer young men in the camp waging war, and it was not because of the casualties. Most of the Comanche men, except for a few of Ten Bears' contemporaries, had disappeared. They were not among the victims on the ground. But neither were they anywhere in sight. It was not until Gabe realized that there were also fewer Apaches in the camp than there had been when they first launched their attack that he knew where the young Comanche men were.

Gone.

The Apaches had taken prisoner the young whom they had not killed, he realized. He fired at an Apache who had just rounded a blazing lodge and started toward him. He missed. Before he could fire again, a tall Apache wearing a white headband and a scarlet sash around his waist and riding a black horse with a blaze gave a shout and then pointed to the south.

Gabe fired again at the Apache he had missed as the man, together with the remaining Apaches in the camp, boarded his horse and went galloping after the man who had shouted the command. Gabe missed again, and by the time he had taken aim in preparation for a third shot, the Apaches were gone from the camp and disappearing in the smoke that trailed in their wake.

He looked around at the devastation and the desolation and felt a chill hand clutch his heart and squeeze it. Likes Horses, he thought. Where?

He began to search the camp, going over it almost inch by inch. He searched too for Sees the Moon. All he found were other people—dead and, in most cases, badly mutilated. One man was without eyes; they lay on the ground by his twisted body. A woman had no breasts beneath her bloodied buckskin clothing; they lay sliced to ribbons some distance from her corpse. The mutilations had had a purpose, Gabe knew. The Apaches had seen to it that the woman, in the hereafter, would not be able to nurse any babies she might bear. The eyeless man would not be able to see to make his way around the abode of the Great Spirit when he entered the afterlife. Gabe swore under his breath. The attackers had not been content with killing their enemies. They had to do more to injure them. They had to make sure, in terms of the Comanches' beliefs, that those enemies were also bound to suffer in the hereafter.

He passed the scalp pole, which had been pulled down and no longer bore any Apache scalps. He passed the drums that would no longer sound at the hands of the drummers, who lay dead and headless beside their silent instruments.

Ten Bears!

He had almost forgotten the old chief. He hurried out of the camp. He found Ten Bears lying facedown halfway between the chokecherry thicket and the river. The sight made his skin crawl. He knelt beside the old man and placed two fingers on his neck. A pulse, faint, beat there. But a pulse nevertheless. He turned the chief over and spoke his name. He chafed the man's arms, his torso, his legs.

Several minutes passed and then Ten Bears regained consciousness.

As he stared up at Gabe, fear flared in his eyes.

"It's me, Chief. Long Rider."

The fear flickered and died.

"What happened to you?" Gabe asked.

"An Apache—it was their leader, Cha-lipun himself—he hit me with his war club and I lost sight of this world."

Gabe helped the chief sit up. Ten Bears rubbed the back of his head. Suddenly, his body stiffened.

"What is it, Chief? Your head hurts?"

"Likes Horses."

"What about her?"

"Now that memory returns—*aaiieeee!*"

"What's the matter, Chief?" Gabe gripped the shoulder of Ten Bears, who had covered his face with his hands and sat rocking back and forth on the ground.

"He took her. Cha-lipun, he took her. I saw her coming from the river. I stood up and shouted to her. I told her to go back, to run away and hide. Maybe if I had kept quiet he would not have seen her. Suddenly, he was beside Likes Horses like an evil spirit that comes out of the air. He caught her by the hair and pulled her to him. I ran to them. I reached for my knife—I had forgotten I had lost it in the fight. Cha-lipun laughed. Then he struck me with his war club and I knew nothing after that."

"They took the young men, Chief."

"Aaiieee!"

"How come you people didn't post guards around the camp in case those Apaches got the notion to get even with you for the attack you made on them?"

"We did have guards," Ten Bears insisted, uncovering his face. "There," he said as he got shakily to his feet. "And over there," he added, pointing in the opposite direction.

Gabe left the chief and strode over to the spot the old man had first pointed out. A dead young man lay there. Dead not of arrows or a lance or from the blow of a war club. The bruises on the man's throat, which were already turning yellow and black, told Gabe how he had died. The man had been strangled to death so that his spirit would not be able to escape from his body and would remain forever imprisoned in the ground when the man was buried, thus denying it access to the spirit land beyond the setting sun. He checked the other spot Ten Bears had indicated and found that sentry had also been strangled.

Mutilation. Strangulation. And death in the dark.

The Apaches had indeed revenged themselves on the Comanches, he thought. The spirits of those who had died in the night might not be able to find their way to the other world because of the darkness.

Gabe returned to where a forlorn Ten Bears was waiting for him. Both men stood in silence as survivors of the Apache attack made their way back into the camp from the places where they had fled for refuge. They appeared stunned with stricken expressions on their faces as they wandered among the fallen. But then, a woman threw back her head and howled her agony to the night sky. She was joined by others, who began to loudly mourn their slain relatives and friends. An old man knelt by the body of an old woman and clasped her corpse to his breast. He rocked back and forth, tears streaming down his cheeks, sobs tearing from his throat.

"We are a dying people," Ten Bears murmured, his voice so low Gabe was hardly able to make out his words. "Our enemies have destroyed us in two ways. They have killed many of us." He gestured toward the dead and dying that littered the campsite and then toward the starry horizon. "And they have taken away our young men so that our tribe cannot increase as it should. They have stolen our future from us.

"My granddaughter is gone and I am afraid I shall never see her again, just as I have never seen the others the Apaches have taken from us in the past. They will sell her to the Comancheros."

As Ten Bears blinked away the tears that were welling in his eyes, Gabe said, "I will go and find her, Chief."

Ten Bears stared hard at him, his sorrowful expression gradually and tentatively giving way to the traces of a hopeful smile. "I wanted to ask you to find Likes Horses and bring her back to me but I did not dare. One does not ask a stranger to do what he should do for himself. But, you see that I am old. My days of following the long and dangerous trails have ended. You see too"—Ten Bears gestured to the old and the children who had survived the attack—"neither can they do what needs to be done now that our young men have been captured and taken from us.

"But, Long Rider, the Apaches are deadly and will kill you if you try to interfere with their plans. I am sure you know that."

Gabe knew that.

Ten Bears hesitated a brief moment and then said, "The Apaches are led by a man named Cha-lipun. Cha-lipun is crafty as the fox and as deadly as the rattlesnake."

"What's this fellow—this Cha-lipun—look like?"

"He is a tall man. He wears his hair in braids. When he was here tonight with his warriors, he wore a red sash and rode a black horse with a white mark on its head."

"I have seen him then." Gabe recalled the Apache aboard the black horse with a blaze who had shouted an order for the other Apaches to leave the camp following the attack. "I will go now and I will see Cha-lipun again."

"Take great care, Long Rider, so that he and his men may do you no harm."

Gabe nodded and left Ten Bears. He made his way among the wailing mourners, who were cutting their hair with knives and using those same knives to slash their arms and legs, as was the custom during the mourning process.

He picked up his gear from the ground next to the pile of smoldering ashes that had once been Ten Bears' lodge and made his way to the corral. There he saddled his roan and then rode out, a solitary figure in the night, heading south after the Apaches and thinking of Likes Horses.

CHAPTER FOUR

Gabe was still thinking about Likes Horses as he continued his southward journey toward the Apache camp. The moon had long since disappeared in the clouds that were filling the night sky and which prevented him from seeing any sign left by the Apaches. But they had headed south when they left the camp, and he recalled Likes Horses having told him that Chief Ten Bears had moved his Antelope Band north to get away from the Apaches. Both facts strongly suggested that the Apache camp was somewhere to the south.

He kept his course with the help of the pole star's position in the sky. It also told him that there were not many hours left in the night. He spurred his horse to urge it into a trot, not wanting to approach the Apache camp in daylight nor, having found it, to be forced to wait to put into action any plan for freeing the Comanche captives taken by the Apaches.

He was almost in the camp before he even realized it. He had heard no sounds from it and, oddly, there were no guards posted around it or any activity or fires in the camp.

He drew rein and sat his saddle, surveying the camp, which consisted of a cluster of shadowy wickiups in the moonless night. They resembled a series of hummocks and seemed as lifeless.

The scene before him confused him and made him uneasy. He had been expecting to find the camp full of activity. He had fully expected to find everyone up and about and happily celebrating the victory the Apaches had won in the Comanche camp. He thought he might come upon a scene of Apaches torturing one or more of their Comanche captives. But this—

Had the camp been abandoned? There was no way to know for sure, but he thought it highly unlikely. Why would the Apache's leave a well-established camp? Simply abandon their wickiups and walk away?

There were no horses in or near the camp, which made Gabe wonder if he were wrong. Maybe the Apaches, for some reason or other, had indeed picked up and left this place. But then, as the moon emerged from a cove of clouds, he spotted the skin of an elk pegged out on the ground and half scraped. Not far away, in front of a neighboring wickiup, a battered iron kettle sat in the ashes of a dead fire.

They wouldn't have just up and gone off without taking what belonged to them, he reasoned. And, if they'd been driven off, there would be evidence of such an event. Damaged or destroyed wickiups. Dead bodies.

An image of the devasted Comanche camp flared in his mind. It brought with it another image—that of Likes Horses. He dismounted and searched the area until he found what he was looking for—a small pebble. He led his horse into the cover afforded by a mature mesquite tree, returned to his previous position, then threw the pebble. It hit its intended target—the wickiup nearest to him—with a snapping sound that was loud in the otherwise quiet night.

Moments later, a woman wrapped in a blanket cautiously emerged from the wickiup and looked around. A naked little boy, barely old enough to walk, came out after her. He didn't look around. He proceeded to relieve himself. After a moment, boy and woman reentered the wickiup.

Gabe hunkered down and watched the camp. He had proved to himself that it was not totally deserted. There were people sleeping in the wickiups—in at least one of them, at any rate. The woman and the little boy. But where were the warriors who had attacked the Comanche camp? Where were their captives? Also asleep somewhere in the camp? He doubted it.

Maybe daylight would reveal the answers to his questions. If not— Well, he would worry about that at some future time. For lack of a better plan, he would wait to see what the new day would bring.

He went back to his horse, stepped into the saddle and rode up the slope of a low bluff that was crowned with shin oaks. He rode in among them and dismounted. Leaving his roan to browse the underbrush, he sat down with his back against one of the trees and, from his sheltered vantage point, continued watching the camp below and the countryside surrounding it.

By the time the light of dawn had begun to color the sky a pale gold, the camp had come to life. Women appeared from out of the wickiups and began to cook the morning meal.

Sleepy children wandered through the camp, dogs at their heels. Old men wrapped in blankets despite the season came out of the wickiups and sat basking in the sun as it began to rise.

Maybe I've got the wrong Apache camp, Gabe thought as he watched the activities taking place below him. He promptly rejected that possibility. This camp was the one— it had to be, for the simple reason—a negative one—that there were no young men in it. The young men of this camp were, without a doubt, he believed, the ones who had raided the Comanche village. The question was: Where were they now?

I should have waited, he told himself. He should have waited until daybreak to set out after Cha-lipun and his men.

That way, in the light of day, he would have been able to see their trail. Instead of just heading south, he would have been able to follow them wherever the hell it was they went.

Another raid? They might have decided to kill two birds with one stone, he thought. Flushed with the success of their attack on Chief Ten Bears' Antelope Band, they might have tried to duplicate their success with one of the other bands of Comanches present in the general area.

The new day's sun was two hours old when Gabe spotted the Apaches being led by Cha-lipun. They were approaching the camp from the northwest. Gabe stood up. Shielding his eyes with one hand, he stared at the approaching group of young men.

Likes Horses was not with them. Neither was Sees the Moon. None of the Comanche captives the Apaches had taken were with the warriors. Gabe's teeth ground together. A muscle in his jaw jumped. A name resounded in his mind.

Comancheros.

The Apaches must have already disposed of their captives he thought. Instead of heading directly back to their camp, they must have headed for wherever the Comancheros had their headquarters. He could think of no other way to explain the absence of captives among the Apaches, who were almost at their camp now.

Shouts of greeting from the people in the camp rose on the quiet morning air. Women ran to greet their men. Old men watched the war party's arrival in silence, perhaps remembering other days when they themselves had been the eagerly welcomed heroes returning home.

The men dismounted, turning their horses over to a few of the women. They talked to those gathered around them. There was much gesturing and much laughter. As Gabe watched, he was able to see that some of the young men were gesturing to show how they had killed and mutilated their enemies during the night just ended.

The reunion finally came to an end. When it did, Chalipun sent four of his men to the fringes of his camp, there to stand guard.

As the men took up their positions, Gabe decided he would take the one on the eastern edge of the camp, forcing him to tell him what they had done with Likes Horses and the other people they captured.

He cautiously made his way out of the trees and then down the eastern side of the bluff, weaving in and out among frost cracked boulders and over rubble that offered unstable footing at best. When he was a little more than halfway down the slope, he dropped down behind a boulder and cautiously watched the Apache below and to his right.

The man yawned. He walked a few paces and then reversed direction. He yawned again.

Easy pickings.

Gabe moved closer to him. He abruptly halted his advance as his foot dislodged a stone that went clattering down the slope. He remained motionless, his head down, his knees practically touching the ground, for several long minutes. Only then did he dare raise his head to see what the Apache guard was doing.

The man was dozing. He had seated himself on the ground and was leaning against the rotten stump of a mesquite, his arms across his knees, his head bowed.

Gabe smiled to himself and drew his knife. He moved closer to the man, taking great pains not to dislodge any more stones that might give his quarry warning of his approach. His caution proved unnecessary. By the time he was within a few yards of the guard, the man was snoring, his forehead resting on his forearms.

Gabe moved closer, placing one foot after the other only after examining the ground in front of him in search of firm footing. When the Apache stirred, Gabe, fearful that the man was about to awaken and see that he was about to be attacked, sprang forward, speedily covering the last few paces. He seized the guard, jerked him to his feet, spun him around, and slammed his left forearm against the Apache's throat. The knife in his right hand—the tip of its sharp blade—touched the Apache's neck, depressing the flesh but not puncturing it.

"Don't yell," Gabe muttered. "You do and you're dead. You got that?"

The Apache grunted.

"Good. Now then. Where's all the Comanches you and your friends ran off with last night?"

The man said nothing.

The tip of Gabe's knife promptly punctured the skin of the man's throat. When it withdrew, a bead of blood blossomed on the man's flesh. Gabe placed the knife on another spot and pressed. Another puncture. More blood.

"Comancheros," the Indian said.

Gabe realized he had been right, but felt no satisfaction and certainly no pleasure over that fact. "Where are the Comancheros?"

He never knew whether the man would have answered his question. Even before the Apache could attempt to do so, a woman shrieked. Gabe turned his head to see her standing only a few feet away with a bowl of food in her hand, obviously the guard's breakfast. She shrieked again, even louder this time. Within seconds it seemed to Gabe that the entire population of the Apache camp, every man, woman and child in it, had surrounded him. He stared at the weapons in the hands of the men. Bows with arrows already fitted to them. War clubs, all of them raised. Two lances, both of them aimed at his gut.

Cha-lipun was standing in the forefront of the mob, a curved hide-peeler's knife that the Mexicans called *media luna* in his hand. "Take Delshay and the white man back to the camp," he ordered. Then he held out his hand.

Gabe knew he had no choice. He released his hold on the man the Apache leader had called Delshay and then handed his knife to Cha-lipun.

"Your gun belt," Cha-lipun said, pointing to it.

Gabe unbuckled it and handed it over. He had no sooner done so than a man behind him gave him an unexpected shove that sent him stumbling forward. The Apache men formed two lines flanking both him and Delshay, who was walking several paces in front of him, and marched both men—both prisoners—back to the camp. There the lines of men dissolved as the Apaches took up strategic positions to prevent the escape of either Gabe or Delshay.

Cha-lipun appeared carrying Gabe's gun belt and with Gabe's knife tucked beneath the scarlet sash he wore around his waist. All eyes, including Gabe's and Delshay's turned to him.

"You," Cha-lipun said sternly and pointed at Delshay, "were to guard the camp. You did not. You allowed yourself to be captured by this white man."

Delshay remained silent, stoically offering no defense.

"Comanches could have attacked us because you did not keep careful watch," Cha-lipun accused, his eyes drilling into Delshay's. "For everything in this life a man must pay in one way or another. For what you have done, you must now pay." Cha-lipun turned to one of the men standing nearby. "Stake him to the ground." To another man, he said, "Bring fire."

"What of the white man?" the second man asked. "What will we do with him?"

"When we have finished with Delshay, it will then be his turn," Cha-lipun answered.

Gabe stiffened. He didn't know for certain what was about to happen, but he did know that it would not be pleasant. He glanced at Delshay, who stood as stiffly as he himself was standing. The man's face was expressionless, even haughty. He's steeling himself, Gabe thought, for whatever's about to happen to him. He wondered if he would be able to match Delshay's stoicism when it came his turn to experience whatever fate Cha-lipun had in store for him.

The fire was brought in the form of several burning brands, which were used to ignite some bark shavings laid in a small pile on the ground. As the man who had brought the brands added fuel to his small fire, other men, using wooden stakes and strips of rawhide, spread-eagled Delshay with his back against the ground.

Cha-lipun's eyes went from Delshay to the fire and then back again. For his part, Delshay stared up at the sky, his lips set in a thin grim line. Cha-lipun gestured peremptorily. The fire-tender rose and approached Delshay. Bending over, he sprinkled wood shavings on the palm of the bound man's left hand. Then he turned and went back to his fire. He extracted a burning brand from it and carried it back to where Delshay lay, still staring silently at the sky.

Gabe watched with growing horror as the man bent and brought the tip of the burning brand into contact with the shavings resting on the palm of Delshay's hand, which was held motionless by the strip of rawhide that bound his wrist to one of the four stakes.

First, there was only a thin tendril of smoke spiraling up from the wood shavings in Delshay's hand. Then there was a faint glimmer of light, which quickly matured into a flame that was first only an inch high. Then, as if by magic, it flared into a column of fire that rose nearly a foot above its source of fuel, which was both wood and flesh.

Gabe's teeth gritted together, making a rasping sound as he stared at the scene before him. His stomach lurched. Bile rose bitter in his throat. He swallowed it down and forced himself to continue watching as he braced himself for Delshay's scream, which he was sure had to come sooner or later.

At first, as the small fire burned in his palm, Delshay did nothing more than twitch his fingers. Then, as more fuel was added to the fire, he closed his eyes, squeezing them tightly together.

Minutes, which seemed like endless hours to Gabe, passed.

A fire was lighted in Delshay's right hand, a twin of the one now smoldering in his left. Soon the fingers on both of Delshay's hands were doing a swift digital dance. They seemed to be trying to seize and extinguish the fires that were charring his flesh, but none of them was able to so much as touch the flames, let alone put them out.

Delshay's scream, when it finally came, was one that iced Gabe's blood. It was quickly followed by a second agonized scream. Delshay desperately tried to wrench his hands free of the stakes but he could not do so. The sinews in his arms grew taut as he fought against his bonds. His body twisted slightly to one side and then to the other, but the rawhide strips kept him almost completely motionless.

Some of the Apache men, women and children sat down on the ground, their legs folded under them as they continued to watch the torture taking place. Cha-lipun, his arms folded across his chest, watched impassively as Delshay continued to scream, saliva spurting from his lips as he did so. Delshay's eyes rolled in his head. At times, Gabe could see only their whites. When the pupils at times rolled down out of the man's head they were unfocused and showed unmistakable signs of shock.

Cha-lipun gestured again to the fire-tender.

The man calmly and methodically proceeded to slash the white cotton trousers Delshay was wearing in order to expose his belly. Then he built a larger fire on the frantically heaving plain of Delshay's sweating stomach.

Sparks shot up from it. Then flames.

Delshay's screams became the howls of a man demented. He continued to howl and scream and then began to blubber senselessly as the fires in his palms were allowed to die out, leaving behind them charred holes through which scorched blue-white bones showed.

Someone among the Apaches snickered. A woman joined the watching throng carrying a bark bowl full of piñon seeds, which she offered to the spectators as Delshay shrilly cursed

Cha-lipun and all the Apache spirits who had betrayed him.

Gabe glanced over his shoulder, seeking a means of escape before Delshay's ghastly fate became his own. If he could break away, get to his horse—

Two scowling Apache men moved closer to him, as if they realized what he was thinking. His eyes dropped to the knife one of them wore in a sheath hanging from his rawhide belt. His gaze shifted to his own knife, which Cha-lipun now wore tucked beneath the sash around his waist.

His attention was drawn back to Delshay when he heard a sharp spitting sound he did not recognize. He grimaced as he realized that what he was hearing was the sputtering of Delshay's blood as the fire burned it.

Five minutes later, Delshay's mutilated body gave up the ghost with a wail that was more poignant than pained. As its sound faded away, Cha-lipun barked an order and pointed to Gabe.

The two men who were standing closest to him seized him by the arms and held him firmly. He tried hard to jerk free of them but was unable to do so. They dragged him to a spot that was only a few feet distant from where Delshay's savaged corpse was lying. As they did so, the Apaches seated on the ground talked volubly among themselves and watched him with keen interest. He knew what they were thinking. Would he be brave? How soon would he, no matter how brave he was at first, begin to scream in agony as the fires that were to consume and then kill him relentlessly devoured his flesh?

He tried to free himself from the men gripping his arms, but their combined strength was too much for him. Within minutes they had forced him to his knees and then down onto the ground on his back. One of the men held his arms, the other his legs, as a third Apache pounded a sharp stake into the ground next to his left wrist.

The third man then seized his wrist, and the Apache who had been holding it released it. The man who had pounded the stake into the ground was about to tie Gabe's wrist to the stake when Gabe twisted his wrist as hard as he could and slipped free of the stake-pounder's grasp. As he did so, Gabe simultaneously jerked his other hand free. He seized the stake and pulled it out of the ground.

As a roar of surprise went up from the rest of the Apaches, Gabe stabbed the man on his left with the stake. The man screamed in pain and tried to wrest the stake from his chest where Gabe had buried it.

Gabe, wasting no time, turned swiftly in the opposite direction and slammed a hard fist into the face of the other Apache, smashing the man's nose and sending blood spurting from it. Then Gabe was sitting up and reaching for the stunned man holding his legs, who was staring with wide eyes at his companions whom Gabe had just attacked.

Gabe seized the man by the hair, pulled him toward him, then gave him a kick in the solar plexus that broke the man's hold on his legs and sent him sprawling backward into the dirt.

With a cry of rage, Cha-lipun sprang forward, drawing his knife—the *media luna* Gabe had noticed earlier—from his sash. At the same moment, the watching Apache men among the spectators, along with the three Apaches who had been trying to spread-eagle their prisoner, lunged at Gabe, their arms reaching, their dark faces contorted with rage.

Gabe brought his right arm down in a chopping motion. It landed on Cha-lipun's wrist. The *media luna* fell to the ground. Before the Apache leader could retrieve it, Gabe jerked his own knife out of Cha-lipun's sash and pressed its sharp tip against the small of the man's back.

"Stop!" he roared.

The advancing horde of Apaches stopped.

"Any one of you make a move toward me, this man dies. You'll probably get me in the end, but not before I kill your chief. And before you can kill me I'll take one or two—or maybe more of you—with me."

Silence then.

The Apaches stood like statues, some of them crouching, some of them still reaching for Gabe. But none of them moved. Neither did Gabe. Neither did Gabe's knife, the point of which continued to press into Cha-lipun's back.

"I'm taking your chief with me," Gabe announced. He began to back away from the mob of angry Apaches facing him. When one of them took a step in his direction, he pressed the tip of his knife's blade deeper into Cha-lipun's back and the chief grunted. That grunt halted Gabe's would-be attacker.

He continued backing away, his free hand on Cha-lipun's shoulder to force the man to accompany him. As he did so, he ordered Cha-lipun to unbuckle the gun belt he had earlier taken from him. The Apache hesitated, but then promptly obeyed Gabe's order when the knife blade bit deeper into his back. A thin trickle of blood began to stain his shirt. Gabe reached around him, took possession of his gun belt and strapped it around his waist. Moving fast, his actions hidden by his captive, who was standing directly in front of him, he returned his knife to the sheath sewn on his holster and then drew his six-gun. Now its barrel instead of the knife pressed against Cha-lipun's back.

Gabe continued backing away. When he reached the edge of the camp, he noticed that several of the people in the crowd that was slowly following him and Cha-lipun had shifted their eyes to his left and then back to him again. He looked in the same direction and, at first, saw nothing. But then he saw a flicker of movement near the thick trunk of a tree. He halted, forcing his prisoner to do the same, his eyes on the sycamore.

An Apache eased out from behind the tree and peered in his direction. When he realized that Gabe had seen him, he raised the lance in his hand. But before he could throw it, Gabe's gun swiveled away from Cha-lipun's back in the direction of the armed Apache. Gabe squeezed off a shot and the round shattered the would-be lance-thrower's right wrist. As the man let out an agonized howl and dropped his lance, Gabe's gun returned to bore into his captive's back.

They continued backing away from the camp until they reached the bluff near where Gabe had overpowered the Apache guard and where his roan still stood.

"I'm going to let you go," he told Cha-lipun. "But first you're going to tell me what you did with the Comanches you captured."

Cha-lipun said nothing.

Gabe thumbed back the hammer of his .44. The click was enough to make Cha-lipun say, "Sold." Cha-lipun stared off into the distance, and the other Apaches who had followed him and Gabe out of the camp watched the proceedings in stony silence.

"Who'd you sell them to?" Gabe asked wanting to verify what Delshay had already told him.

"Comancheros."

"Now, I've got one more question for you. Where are the Comanchero's holed up?"

"Holed up?"

"Gone to ground. Where's their headquarters?"

"They have a place in the Davis Mountains." Cha-lipun then told Gabe where to find the place he had mentioned.

Gabe stepped away from his prisoner. Still holding his gun in his right hand, he swung into the saddle, said, "Adios," and went galloping away from the spot, leaving the Apaches behind.

But the Apaches did not stay behind. Before Gabe had gone so much as a mile, some of them had returned to their camp, gotten their horses, and had set out in pursuit of him, with Cha-lipun aboard his black leading the chase.

Gabe glanced over his shoulder as he rode and saw them coming after him through the dust his racing roan was raising. They looked like dusky apparitions, their outlines blurred by the dust through which they were riding. They whooped as they rode, their voices loud and threatening. All of them brandished weapons—bows, lances, war clubs.

Gabe turned and fired at them. An Apache riding to the left and slightly behind Cha-lipun went down. The man's horse ran on and then swerved to one side and stopped. The other Apaches continued the pursuit. Gabe fired again. This time he missed. His third shot shattered the skull of Cha-lipun's black. Where once was the black's blaze, there was now a crater of broken bone bathed in blood. The horse went down, throwing its rider. Several Apaches who had been riding directly behind their leader went down as well as their mounts skittered over the dead black.

Gabe galloped on. An occasional quick glance over his shoulder revealed to him that the Apaches had halted their pursuit. He slowed his horse and let go of the reins. As the horse raced on, he thumbed cartridges out of his belt and filled the three empty chambers of his gun. He had no sooner done so than he heard the sound of pounding hooves behind him. Picking up his reins, he spurred his roan and looked back over his shoulder.

The Apaches had resumed their pursuit of him. All of them had, that is, except one who remained on foot behind the others. Gabe realized that the buckskin Cha-lipun was now riding must have been confiscated from the man left behind. He quickly reconnoitered the area and then headed for a stand of trees that lay off to his right. He fired several rapid rounds at his pursuers but none, to his consternation, did any damage.

He holstered his gun and raked the flanks of his horse with his spurs. The roan responded with a renewed burst of speed that took horse and rider into the stand of lodgepole pines and out of sight of the pursuing Apaches. Gabe stood up in his stirrups, let go of his reins, and seized the first low-hanging branch he came to with both hands. He pulled himself up onto it as his horse galloped on and disappeared among the trees. He quickly climbed higher into the pine tree until he reached a spot where he believed himself to be safely hidden from sight.

Within minutes, the Apache horde thundered by beneath the tree in which he perched. He could hear them better than he could see them because of the thickly needled branches below him. In moments they were gone. He waited, knowing they would be back when they found his horse and learned that he had eluded them. They would spend some time searching for sign of him but, when they found none, they would, he hoped, give up their hunt for him.

He heard them returning before he was able to catch his first glimpse of them through the branches. They were riding slowly now as they talked among themselves and continued searching for sign of him. Occasionally one of the party would veer sharply away from the others and search the area on one of the group's flanks. Finding nothing, the man would rejoin his companions and travel on with them.

Gabe remained absolutely motionless and held his breath as the Apaches passed beneath the tree where he had taken refuge. He stood, precariously balanced on a limb, his right arm tightly wrapped around the tree's trunk to steady himself, his gun cocked in his left hand and aimed downward. None of the Apaches looked up into the tree. When they were gone, Gabe made himself wait a good ten minutes in case they had sent out scouts who might return to the main party, or in case there were any stragglers among the group. When he was finally satisfied that it would be safe to climb down to the ground, he did so, falling at one point when he misjudged his steps and a branch broke beneath his boots. He managed to catch hold of another branch and, for a moment, he swung in mid-air before finally finding a sturdier branch to stand on as he continued his descent.

Once on the ground, he went in search of his horse. At least, he thought as he walked through the forest, the Apaches didn't decide to take my roan and my gear. He had known that was a possibility when he had conceived his escape plan. But he had decided then and believed now that what he had done was the only thing he could have done that might let him escape from the Apaches, even though his action placed his property at risk.

He followed the trail the Apaches had left both going and coming, knowing it would eventually lead him to his mount. It did. He halted and stared down at the body of the roan, which lay on the ground on its left side, its front legs bent as if it were sleeping. Its great black eyes stared sightlessly at nothing. Flies and ants had settled on the gaping knife wound in the animal's neck.

The Apaches must have known he'd come to get his horse sooner or later after giving them the slip. He swore under his breath.

Resigning himself to accepting what he could not change, he went to his dead horse and, after unbuckling his cinch strap and doing some heavy tugging and pulling, he managed to free his saddle. He removed the horse's bridle, stirring up a swarm of flies, which buzzed about his face before resettling on the horse's slashed throat to resume feasting in competition with the ants.

Slinging his saddle, rifle and the rest of his gear over his shoulder, Gabe began to walk through the stand. His passage startled a flock of grackles, which went winging up into the sky above him. A chipmunk chattered its annoyance at his presence. When he emerged from the trees some time later, the Davis Mountains were within sight. He headed south toward them.

Hours later, he had begun to wend his way through a twisting canyon that would, according to the directions he had been given by Cha-lipun, ultimately lead him to the headquarters of the Comancheros. His heart stirred within him when he thought of Likes Horses and how close he was to her at the moment. Excitement surged within him as he thought about freeing her and Sees the Moon and the other Comanche captives being held by the Comancheros.

But how to free them?

He didn't know the answer to his question. Maybe he could sneak up on the place under cover of darkness and stealthily release the Comanche prisoners. Maybe he could—

He deliberately set his thoughts aside. He wouldn't know what he could—or couldn't—do until he surveyed the Comancheros' headquarters and the surrounding area. He quickened his pace as if he had heard Likes Horses call his name and ask for his help.

CHAPTER FIVE

The headquarters of the Comancheros came into sight as Gabe emerged from the canyon through which he had been walking into a wide valley with steep slopes to the east and west, which were partially covered by mesquite and ocotillo bushes. It consisted of a long sod ranch house that had glass windows set into its front wall at widely spaced intervals and a pine door painted blue.

There was a pole-snake fence surrounding the ranch building, which was in disrepair. Parts of it had fallen to the ground in places. To the left of the ranch and some distance from it stood a building that Gabe guessed served as a barn. He noted the armed man standing in front of its door. A place for prisoners? Near it was a smaller outbuilding. Through its open door Gabe could see tack scattered on the floor and hanging on its walls. A post corral containing an assortment of horses was behind the ranch and its gate was in need of repair. Near it was another sod structure, which Gabe took to be a bunkhouse because of the cracked mirror that was fastened with wire to the wall to the left of the door, the wash basin sitting on a bench below it, and the dirty rag that apparently served as a towel hanging on a nail next to the mirror.

That pole fence, Gabe thought, was put up to slow anybody down who might have a notion to come riding hell-for-leather up to this place, though a determined man aboard a good horse might manage to jump over it. The place looked like the average homesteader's ranch, but there were things about it that strongly suggested to Gabe that the people living in the buildings were not homesteaders. There was no vegetable garden growing near the ranch. No chickens scratched in the dirt. There were no curtains on any of the windows. No house cat basked in the rays of the descending sun and no dog prowled about among the buildings. The place definitely lacked most of the common signs of ordinary domesticity.

Gabe started toward the ranch, but had not gone more than four feet when a male voice behind him barked, "Drop your gun and raise your hands!"

Gabe halted. He let his saddle and other gear slide from his shoulder to the ground. He took his Colt out of its holster and dropped it. He raised his hands.

The man who had given him the order walked around to face him, a scowl on his weathered face and two Navy Colts in his hands. "Just what the hell do you think you're doing here?"

"Now what kind of a welcome is this?" Gabe asked, beginning to grin, although he was not feeling at all amused by this latest development. But his easy manner just might make the man taking aim at him ease off some.

It didn't. The man continued to scowl. His drooping black mustache, which was stained in places with tobacco juice, twitched. "I'm waiting to hear you tell your story, mister," he said.

Gabe glanced over his shoulder. A dapple stood about thirty yards behind him. He hadn't heard the horse approach.

I'm slipping, he thought. I keep this up and I won't live out my normal life span.

He said, "My name's Conrad. Gabe Conrad. I heard tell of this place and I thought I'd mosey out and see if what I heard about it's true."

"What did you hear about it?"

"That it shelters a bunch of boys who call themselves Comancheros. But hold on a minute. Are you the padrone of this place?"

The man shook his head. "That would be Miguel Camargo. I'm his right-hand man. Sid Vickers is the name."

"Now, I don't mean no offense, Vickers, but if you don't mind I'd rather tell my tale to your boss than to you. He inside the ranch there?"

"He is."

"Then I'll go talk to him, what do you say?"

"I'll be right behind you."

"You mean I should leave my belongings out here?"

"March, Conrad."

Gabe marched in the direction of the ranch. "Can I put my hands down now?"

Vickers didn't answer so Gabe played it safe. He kept his hands in the air. Halfway to the ranch, he asked, "Where'd you come from, Vickers?"

"I was up on the mesa with a spyglass. It was my turn to stand guard. I saw you coming and rode down off the mesa and up behind you."

"You sure did move silent as any snake—no offense meant. I'm just saying I didn't hear a peep out of you or your horse till you were nearly on top of me."

Gabe stopped in front of the blue door of the ranch.

"Open it," Vickers ordered.

Gabe did. He lowered his hands and stepped into a large room made dim by the fact that light had difficulty penetrating the grimy windows.

"Got us a visitor, Camargo," Vickers announced from behind Gabe.

Camargo, seated in a cane-backed wooden chair, was a wiry man, all sinew and no soft spots. His hair was straight and long and black as death. So was the thick mustache he wore that hid his upper lip. He had razored sideburns that reached halfway down his sunken cheeks, and penetrating black eyes that seemed to pierce whatever they looked at.

He wore a pair of flared velvet trousers the color of a winter sunset and a silk shirt as blue as any sky. Over his shirt he wore a colorfully embroidered vest. Two .45 caliber Remington revolvers hung from a cartridge belt that rode high on his hips.

He picked up a battered pot and poured coffee into a tin cup. He took a drink of the coffee, rolled it around in his mouth, then spat it out on the dirt floor.

"Swill," he said. He muttered an oath and then glanced in Gabe's direction. His eyes appraised his visitor for a long moment and then, to Vickers, he said, "He looks like a choirboy. Who is he?"

"Says his name's Gabe Conrad," Vickers replied. "Spotted him on his way through the canyon and followed him in. He was on foot. His gear's outside."

"What's he want?"

Gabe felt mild annoyance at the way Camargo was talking about him as if he were unable to speak for himself.

"I don't know," Vickers answered. "Said he wanted to talk to you."

"Well, Choirboy, talk."

"I'm not a man who enjoys beating about the bush, Camargo," Gabe began. "So I'll say it plain and I'll say it straight. I've come to throw in with you and your boys."

Camargo's eyebrows arched. His eyes widened. He took a fat cigar from his pocket, struck a wooden match and lit it. Blowing a thick cloud of smoke in Gabe's direction, he asked, "Why?"

"Why do I want to join your outfit? On account of I've heard tell it's the top one around and I only ride for top men. That's why."

"What do you know about this outfit, Choirboy?"

"My name's Conrad, not Choirboy."

"Touchy fellow, aren't you, Choirboy?"

Gabe was about to insist that Camargo call him by his rightful name rather than the obviously mocking appelation Choirboy, but he resisted the impulse, telling himself it didn't matter what he was called. What did matter was why he was here and what he hoped to accomplish before he finally left.

"I asked you a question."

Vickers, from behind Gabe, said, "Camargo wants to know what and how much you know about us."

"I know you're Comancheros," Gabe said. "I know you deal in stolen cattle and horses. Sometimes in stolen people."

Camargo's eyebrows dropped down as he frowned. "You want to be a bad boy too, is that it?"

"You could put it that way," Gabe declared.

Camargo nodded. "You don't look like a horse thief. Are you a horse thief, Choirboy?"

"I've stolen a horse or two in my time."

"But at the moment you find yourself on foot. Why is that?" Camargo wanted to know as he blew a series of perfect smoke rings.

"I had some trouble back along the trail a ways. I ran into some Apaches. They didn't get me but they did get my horse."

"Are you afraid of Apaches?"

"I can hold my own with them, I reckon."

"I ask the question because if you should become one of us—but, mind you, I am the one who will decide if you will or will not, and I have not yet made up my mind—you will meet Apaches from time to time. They are—how shall I put it?—business associates of ours."

Gabe waited for Camargo to go on.

"They frequently take prisoners in their battles with other Indian tribes. They bring them here to us and we buy them for a suitable fee, which usually takes the form of bad whiskey and some trade beads and trinkets. So if you are afraid of Apaches, you will not be happy here."

"Camargo, why don't you stop all this dancing around the mulberry bush and let's see if we can't make a deal on a man-to-man basis. What do you say to that suggestion?"

Up went Camargo's eyebrows again in feigned surprise. "I was just trying to get to know you, Choirboy. But, as you say, it is time to deal. Now then, you say you want to ride with us. How will you do that without a horse to call your own?"

"I figured I'd buy one from you if you've got any to spare."

"As it happens, I do have a horse I'd be willing to sell you—for a fair price. But hold on. I'm getting ahead of myself here. First, I have to know whether you have the proper qualities to be a Comanchero. Would you be willing to take a little test so that I might see if you have the nerve and the guts you'll need to be one of us?"

"I'll take—and pass—any test you can come up with," Gabe stated firmly without a moment's hesitation. "What'd you have in mind?"

"Come outside," Camargo said, rising and beckoning to him. "I'll show you what I have in mind."

Gabe and Vickers followed Camargo outside, where the Comanchero leader said, "You stand there, Choirboy." He pointed to a spot midway between the ranch and Gabe's pile of gear.

"What have you got in mind for me, Camargo?" Gabe asked.

"Understand something," an unsmiling Camargo barked, his eyes glittering as he gazed sternly at Gabe. "When I give you an order, you don't ask me questions about it. You obey. That is, if you wish to be one of my men."

Gabe, without another word, went to the spot Camargo had indicated and stood there without speaking.

"Vickers will test you, Choirboy," Camargo called out to Gabe. "He will show you a trick I saw performed for the first time below the border by some Apaches. It is a way to test a man's nerve in the face of grave danger. Vickers will ride down on your position. He will come close to you at times. Uncomfortably close. If you move—if you even shift your feet so much as one little inch—you can pick up your gear and walk out of here and that will be the end of the matter. If, on the other hand, you can manage to stand your ground—then we will see. Then maybe you will not be a choirboy anymore. Then you may be one of us—a Comanchero."

Camargo signaled to Vickers, who was once again in the saddle, and the man walked his horse a hundred yards to the east of where Gabe was standing.

"Is your man Vickers a good horseman?" Gabe asked Camargo.

"He is good, yes. I know what you are thinking. You are thinking that he might lose control of his horse and make mincemeat out of you. That is so, yes?"

"It's so, yes."

Camargo shrugged. "What can I say? Unfortunately accidents do happen."

Gabe turned to face Vickers, who was sitting his saddle in the distance. A moment later, as Camargo gave a signal, Vickers spurred his horse and came galloping toward Gabe as he stiffly stood his ground.

He wanted to close his eyes but he would not permit himself to do so. He stared at the oncoming dapple and, as the animal came rapidly close to him, he seemed to see only its great eyes and its wet white teeth, which were bared as a result of Vickers' hard hold on the reins.

The horse went pounding past him on the right with no more than a foot between itself and Gabe. He imagined he could feel the heat of the animal's body as it galloped past him. He swallowed hard as Vickers wheeled his mount and rode away. He waited, watching as Vickers again wheeled his mount and started galloping back toward him again. The thunder of the horse's hooves seemed to Gabe like the loudest sound he had ever heard in his life. As eight hundred pounds of horse bore down on him, he longed to give in to his almost overpowering impulse to run for his life in any direction so long as it was away from the oncoming horse and rider.

He saw the sadistic grin on Vickers' face as he came closer. He saw the saliva spraying from the horse's mouth. He saw the sheen of sweat glistening on the animal's great body.

As the horse approached, he stood without moving a muscle, his eyes wide open, his heart pounding against his ribs as if it would at any moment break through the bony barrier that imprisoned it and burst out into the open.

Gabe almost cried out as Vickers suddenly swerved and seemed to be heading directly for him. But he didn't. Instead, he clenched his fists at his sides and continued to stand his ground as Vickers swerved again—but just seconds too late to avoid colliding with Gabe. As the man's horse turned sharply, its head drawn back by the bit in its mouth as Vickers gave it a hard jerk, its right flank slammed against Gabe and knocked him to the ground.

He immediately got up again and took up his position as before. Out of the corner of his eye he could see Camargo watching him. If he had expected the leader of the Comancheros to call a halt to the dangerous proceedings, he was disappointed. Vickers rode away from him, wheeled his mount and headed back toward him again.

This time—Vickers' third pass—almost broke Gabe's nerve. He almost ran. Feeling the growing ache in his right arm and shoulder, the result of having just been struck by Vickers' dapple, he knew there were worse things that could happen to him. The horse's flying hooves might— He wouldn't let himself complete the thought. He didn't blink as Vickers slammed past him with only inches to spare. The dapple's sweat and saliva struck Gabe's face as the horse passed him. He kept his hands at his sides, not bothering to wipe away the wetness as he watched Vickers return once more to his starting point.

"Enough!" Camargo shouted.

Relief as sweet as water to a man in a desert swept over Gabe. It was over at last. He slowly turned his head toward Camargo as he approached him.

"Not bad," the Comanchero leader declared offhandedly when he reached Gabe. "Not bad at all. I'll forgive your fall—chalk it up to your inexperience at playing Apache games."

"I take it then that I am now officially a Comanchero," Gabe said.

Camargo raised an index finger and waggled it at him. "Not so fast. You passed the first test. Now we have to see if you can pass the second test before we officially welcome you to our organization."

"Wait a minute, I—"

"You will do as I say or you will not remain here!" an angry Camargo bellowed, bringing a sly smile to the face of Vickers, who had just joined them.

Gabe swallowed his pride and asked, What's this second test you're talking about?"

"I want to see if you are a skilled horse thief. There are, my scouts report, some soldiers from Fort Stockton bivouaced west of here. They are trying to round up Apaches who have been attacking the fort of late. The soldiers have fine horses with them, my scouts say. You will go and find the soldiers and steal their horses from them and bring them back here."

"You're expecting me to steal horses from the United States Army?" an incredulous Gabe asked.

"You do not think you can pass such a test, eh?"

Camargo had him and Gabe knew it. "I'll need a horse if I'm to try to pass your test."

"Ah, yes, of course. I have just the horse for you. For you I have the king of horses. Come, I will show him to you."

Camargo led the way to the corral with Gabe and Vickers following him. When they reached the corral, Camargo hooked a boot heel on one of the enclosure's poles and pointed to a gray. "That one should suit you. He stands thirteen hands high and he has the wind of a cyclone. He's only four years old. I hate to part with him. He's a favorite of mine. But for you—take him."

"How much?"

"Forty dollars."

"He looks to me to be worth about fifteen."

"You insult this king of horses, Choirboy!"

Gabe had had enough. "My name's Conrad. Maybe you forgot. Maybe you have a short memory. But now that I've refreshed it, I expect you'll remember. Am I right about that, Camargo?"

"Whatever you say." Camargo made an aimless gesture as he avoided the stony stare Gabe was giving him. Turning to Vickers, he said, "Saddle the gray and show Choir— Conrad what he can do."

The two men waited while Vickers did as he had been told. Then Camargo opened the gate of the corral and Vickers, aboard the gray, rode out and spurred the animal. Gabe watched carefully as the horse raced away from the corral. He was still watching five minutes later, when Vickers had returned to the corral.

"I'd like to ride him myself if you don't mind," Gabe said as Vickers stepped down from the saddle.

"You want—" Camargo spluttered. "But you just saw how this horse can run. Like the wind, he runs. So—"

Ignoring Camargo, Gabe swung aboard the gray and raked its flanks with his spurs. The horse shot forward. They had covered no more than one-quarter of a mile when the gray suddenly slowed, almost stopping in its tracks. Gabe touched it lightly with his spurs. The horse tried valiantly to respond to the goading but failed to do so. Gabe walked the animal back to where Camargo and Vickers were waiting beside the corral.

"He's no good, Camargo," Gabe said as he slid out of the saddle. "I figured as much when I saw how he slowed down after getting a fast start when Vickers rode him. You fellows were trying to pull an old trick on me but it didn't work."

"What the hell are you talking about?" Vickers grunted.

Camargo held up a hand to quiet the man. "What seems to be the problem, Conrad?"

Gabe patted the gray's neck. "This horse is broken winded. He'll give a spurt and then peter out in no time at all because he's not got good wind. You're welcome to him. I don't want him."

"I can tell you've done some horse-trading in your day, Conrad," Camargo said with a slick smile. "Tell you what I'll do. I'll sell you that bay in there for thirty dollars. Take a look at him. Take a good look. Tell me what you think."

Gabe entered the corral and, shouldering his way through the horses it contained, made his way over to the bay. When he reached it, he checked its coat. No scars or bruises, which meant that the horse wasn't subject to blind staggers or to rolling and tumbling about during attacks of colic. He found no cotton in the ears when he examined them but, just to be sure the horse wasn't noise-shy, he walked around behind it and then clapped his hands together. At the sound of the loud report, the horse did nothing more than swing its head around to stare at Gabe.

Later, when he had completed his inspection of his prospective purchase, he left the corral, retrieved his gear and got the bay ready to ride. He gave it a ten-minute workout, and when it ended and he was satisfied, he rode back to the corral and told Camargo he'd buy the horse from him—for twenty dollars. They settled, after haggling for nearly ten minutes, on twenty-five dollars and the sale was made.

"I suggest you go now to steal the soldier boys' horses from them—if you can," Camargo said. "The night is best for such evil deeds, eh? But, before you go, I imagine you have not eaten a good meal in some time."

"You imagine right on the money."

"Then come inside and we will have something to eat. That way you will maintain your strength for the task that faces you. There is whiskey inside as well. It will strengthen your nerve."

"I don't need any whiskey for that."

Camargo made a dismissive gesture. "Have it your way. Come."

Leaving Vickers behind them, Camargo and Gabe made their way back to the ranch. Once inside it, Camargo clapped his hands and, in response, a young Indian woman appeared from a room at the rear of the building.

"Bring food, woman," Camargo ordered her. "Bring it quickly."

When the woman had disappeared, Gabe said, "I take it she's one of your Indian prisoners. A Comanche?"

"She is Apache," Camargo said, offering Gabe a cigar, which was refused. "The Comanches attack the Apaches and vice versa. In both cases, I am the beneficiary of their warmaking. I gain merchandise as a result, like the woman you just saw. She is not the best of cooks but she can make a man's bed bounce and keep him well-satisfied." Camargo lit his cigar and blew smoke into the room.

The woman returned sometime later bearing a platter of pancakes and a pot of coffee. From a cupboard she took a crock of honey and placed it on the table.

As he dug into the meal to end the hunger that had been growing within him for some time now, Gabe asked, "Where do you keep your captives?"

"In the barn under guard."

"Have you had this place long?"

"Not long. Six months. We drove off the family who owned it. They were refugees from the hardscrabble life below the border." Camargo used his fingers to fold a pancake into a small square, dip it in the honey and then stuff it into his mouth. "That's the way to get on in the world, Conrad," he said around his mouthful of food, his words hard to understand. "When you see what you want—be it money, a ranch like this one, a woman—take it and kill or maim anybody who tries to stop you from doing so. A simple course of action but a direct and, I have found, highly effective one."

"You got any prisoners out in the barn at the moment?"

"My men," Camargo said, washing down what food remained in his mouth with coffee, "they have returned." He rose from the table and went to the window. "They have more merchandise with them. We shall all be rich men before long if this keeps up," he concluded with a broad smile before leaving the ranch house to greet the newcomers.

Gabe hungrily devoured the last of his meal and then followed him outside.

Camargo was eagerly greeting the two men—one a Mexican, one an Indian—who had ridden up to the ranch with a small herd of cattle traveling ahead of them. All of the stock was branded, Gabe noted, and also earmarked. The two men's clothes were nondescript and none too clean.

"Who the hell's he?" the Mexican asked, pointing to Gabe.

"He," Camargo replied, "is—or I should say hopes to be—a new recruit. You, Sanchez, will, if he makes the grade, take him under your wing and teach him how to cut men's throats and tumble women, eh?"

The Indian snickered.

"He goes to find the soldier boys tonight," Camargo continued. "He will bring us back fine horses, if the soldiers do not kill him first."

"This gringo, he is crazy, si?" mocked Sanchez, who had a scar that partially closed his right eye. "No one but an Indian like our amigo, Cuchillo, can steal horses form soldiers on bivouac because those smart gringos, they tie their horses to their wrists with rawhide when they sleep." The man laughed, the sound a cracked cackle, and pointed a finger at Gabe. "Maybe the gringo, he bring back horses—*and* the soldiers tied to them!"

Camargo said, "How he steals the army's horses is his problem. But if he does succeed in stealing some and bringing them back here, then he will join our band and become one of us. That is the bargain I have made with him, and I am a man of my word who honors bargains honorably made."

"We do not need more men," Cuchillo grumbled. "More men means we each get less of the money we get for what we steal. Send him away."

"Be at ease, Cuchillo. There is enough for all of us and soon there will be more. I have plans. Now, you and the others put these cows out to pasture. Post a guard to look after them. Go!"

When the two men had gone, driving the cattle before them, Camargo confided, "Cuchillo, he is a Tonto Apache. A good man in a fight but one who tends to be greedy, as are so many of his kind. Still, he serves me well. As I hope you will too, Conrad."

Gabe recognized the implicit order in Camargo's last remark. "I'll be seeing you," he said and went to where he had left his newly purchased bay. He swung into the saddle, nodded curtly to Camargo and rode north away from the ranch. As he passed the barn and the man guarding it, he heard the sound of a woman weeping within it. Likes Horses?

He thought of the task facing him—to steal horses from a bunch of soldiers who would have sentries patrolling the night. It would, he knew, be no easy task to accomplish. But he also knew that he would do his damnedest to accomplish it. Everything depended now on his passing this second test that Camargo had set for him. He had to succeed at it. Because if he failed, he would be ousted by Camargo, and thus have little or no chance of saving the Comanche captives from whatever ugly fate awaited them at the hard hands of the Comancheros.

He rode with the moon that raced through the sky past trees that caught the stars in their leafy nets and across barren wastelands where nothing but cacti grew. He scanned the ground around him as he rode, searching for sign of soldiers. When he found none, he altered his course, crisscrossing the countryside as he continued his search.

The moon sailed on when he stopped and surveyed what had clearly been a campground. The dirt was torn up by men's boots and horses' hooves. There were the ashes of a fire that no longer burned or even smoldered. There were horse droppings everywhere, making Gabe wonder why this particular troop of cavalry didn't picket their horses—or confine them under guard in a rope corral—some distance from the camp itself. Then he recalled Sanchez's mocking remarks about his impending attempt at horse-stealing. The soldiers kept their horses with them, he thought. Every man jack of them did. Tied to them, no doubt, like Sanchez said. He clucked to his bay and the horse moved out. Maybe I will wind up with some soldiers to take back to the Comancheros along with their horses. The thought made him grin.

It was several hours later when the trail he had been following from the campsite led him to the new camp the troopers had established near the bank of a stream and on the edge of a thin growth of mesquite trees. He drew rein and sat his saddle, staring at the dying fire still burning in the center of the camp and giving off the fragrant odor of mesquite, and at the soldiers sleeping on the ground, each man's horse tied to his wrist with a length of rawhide.

His alert eyes picked out the two sentries patrolling the perimeter of the camp. He also spotted the lupine and brittle-bush growing on the eastern edge of the camp. He stepped down from the saddle and, leaving his horse ground-hitched, made his stealthy way around the perimeter of the camp, carefully keeping his distance from the two patrolling sentries as he did so. When he reached the stand of brittle-bush, he gathered some leaves from the plants. Then, carrying two handfuls of the foliage, he got down on his belly and snaked his way toward the spot where the nearest trooper lay blissfully sleeping.

No, not so blissfully sleeping. The man stirred and stretched while Gabe lay frozen on the ground, not moving so much as an eyelid.

The trooper mumbled something. Soon the man was snoring, the sounds seeming to lull his horse, which stood in the moonlit darkness staring dully at Gabe, who had raised his head and was looking around the camp. When he was satisfied that his presence had not been detected, he slithered around the sleeping trooper and offered some of the brittle-bush foliage to the horse. When the animal took it, its upper lip rippling and its teeth gleaming white in the light of the night's moon, Gabe drew his knife. Slowly, carefully, he sliced through the rawhide thong that circled the chewing horse's neck and ran down to the trooper's right wrist. It gave way. As it did, Gabe caught the loose wrist-end so that it would not fall and strike the man's hand. He lowered it to the ground, stood up, gripped the other end of the rawhide and led the horse out of the camp and into the stand of Brittle-bush, where the horse eagerly began to browse. Then, dropping down on his belly again, he eased his body crablike along the ground, this time toward another trooper and that man's drowsy horse. When he reached the animal he remained bellied down on the ground, since this man was sleeping in the thin light still being shed by the dying camp fire, and sliced through the rawhide that bound the horse to the soldier. He repeated the process of leading the horse to the browse of brittle-bush and then, praying his luck would hold, returned to the camp on his belly and freed a third horse.

He had almost reached the thick stand of brittle-bush when he heard one of the two sentries approaching. Leaving the horse behind him and crouching low, he ran as lightly as he could across the lengthy expanse of ground that separated him from the other two browsing horses. He dropped down out of sight among the brittle-bush as behind him he heard the sentry mutter, "Now, what in hell's hot name is this?"

Separating the plants and peering through them, Gabe watched the sentry stand staring at the third freed horse from whose neck the severed rawhide dangled.

The sentry shouldered his carbine and walked around the horse, shaking his head in consternation as he did so. He picked up the dangling rawhide and, still shaking his head, led the horse back to the camp and the trooper from whom Gabe had just stolen it. The sentry bent over and shook the sleeping soldier. A muted discussion followed with the sentry gesturing to the horse as he held up the dangling length of rawhide.

Time to bid this place good-bye, Gabe said to himself. He knew that any second now one or the other of the pair was going to have the good sense to examine that rawhide and figure out it didn't break because it was rotted but because somebody cut it. He shot to his feet and, placing his right hand on one horse's rump and his left shoulder on the other's, he manhandled both of them, despite their reluctance to leave the rich browse, away from the camp and toward the spot where he had left his bay.

When he reached the animal, he glanced back over his shoulder in the direction of the low-burning camp fire, which glowed orange in the moon's white light. He could no longer see the sentry or the soldier with whom he'd been talking. Were they out there in the night somewhere searching for him? He didn't wait to find out. He proceeded to tie the ends of the rawhide loops to his saddle horn, placing one horse on either side of his bay. Then, with some slight difficulty due to the nearness of the soldiers' horses to the body of his bay, stepped into the saddle and walked his horse away from the distant camp as quietly as he could.

He stiffened as one of the three horses stepped on a downed tree limb and it snapped. The sound seemed to Gabe like thunder in the night. Would it bring the soldiers to apprehend him? He moved on, his bay trotting now, the other two horses keeping pace.

No soldiers appeared. No cries of alarm were raised in the camp that he was leaving far behind him. He let out the breath he had not even realized he had been holding and spurred his bay into a gallop. The bodies of the army mounts on either side of him slammed against his legs from time to time, and he wondered if the end of his journey would find him limping. But he endured the punishment as a necessary price he had to pay to achieve his goal.

With his thoughts filled with images of the attack that the Apaches had launched on the Comanche camp, which had ended with the taking of the prisoners he had promised Chief Ten Bears to free, he rode on. As the first light of false dawn lightened the sky and banished the moon from sight, he rode through the canyon and into the Comanchero camp.

The first thing that struck him as he rode toward the ranch house was the silence of the place. The second was that there was no guard posted now in front of the barn where the captives were imprisoned.

To hell with the horses I stole, he thought. Now's the time to get inside that barn while there's nobody around and then get the hell out of here with the people inside it before Camargo or any of his men are any the wiser.

He quickly untied the two army horses from his saddle horn and then headed for the barn. Before he reached it, a rifle shot rang out, sending sharp echoes swirling through the area. He turned and looked behind him. Up on the mesa on the left side of the canyon stood Sanchez with a rifle in his hands. Sanchez smiled and gave him a wave.

Cursing under his breath, Gabe returned both the smile and the wave. He had no sooner done so than a sleepy Camargo, his hair tousled and his eyes puffy, appeared in the doorway of the ranch house and said in a whiskey-coarsened voice, "So you are back."

As Camargo left the house, Vickers emerged from the bunkhouse, obviously alerted to Gabe's arrival by Sanchez's signaling shot.

"You only got two horses?" Vickers questioned Gabe. "That's all you have to show for the night's work, two horses?"

"Shut up, Vickers," Camargo said. Turning to Gabe, he asked, "Were the horses tied to their owners?"

"With rawhide, as you can see," Gabe replied.

"See, Vickers," an obviously pleased Camargo crowed. "Our friend, Conrad, has pulled a slick trick and I imagine the soldier boys think some Indian made off with their mounts."

In a sense, Gabe thought to himself, an Indian did. The Oglalas were the ones who taught him how to steal horses from the bluecoats and not get caught.

"Vickers," Camargo said, "take those two horses Conrad has brought us and put them in the corral. Conrad, you deserve a drink to celebrate the successful conclusion of your night's work, and I need a hair of the dog, as you gringos say."

As Gabe walked with Camargo toward the ranch, he said, "I don't mean to mind your business for you, but I noticed when I rode in here this morning that there's nobody guarding your Indian captives in the barn back there."

"You're right on that score," Camargo commented nonchalantly.

"Aren't you afraid they might try to escape?"

"They're gone."

"Gone?"

"We sold them last night while you were off on your horse-stealing expedition. That's why I have such a hangover this morning. We did some drinking while haggling over prices with our clients and one thing led to another. *Mio Dios*, my head feels like it is going to explode at any minute."

A bitter blend of disappointment and frustration swept over Gabe as he followed Camargo into the ranch house.

CHAPTER SIX

"Here, have some of this," Camargo said, handing Gabe a glass that was half full of brandy. "That stuff's imported from Spain. We stole it along with a whole lot of other goods from a wagon train a few weeks ago down on the Rio Bravo. Drink up, Conrad. That stuff'll put hair on your chest and lead in your pencil."

Gabe took the glass but didn't drink from it. "Did you get a good price for the Indians you sold while I was away?"

"Good enough."

"How do you go about selling the Indians? I mean, you don't advertise in newspapers, do you?"

"We put out the word that we have people for sale. Or cattle. Or horses. We have a core of more or less steady customers. Like those that were here last night. I'd sent word by one of my men to potential buyers that we have what they might well be looking for and told them if they were interested to show up last night. Most of them did, with the welcome result that we sold off every last one of those Comanches we traded with the Apaches for."

"Who do you sell such captives to?" Gabe asked, continuing his probing as he sought to find out what had happened to the Comanche prisoners, especially Likes Horses and Sees the Moon.

"To mine owners mostly. They're always in need of laborers. There are a bunch of mines in Texas and over in Arizona Territory. Gold mines and such. Working in them is hard work. It wears a man down fast. So the mine owners keep coming back to me for fresh workers to replace those who die or become injured so badly they can't work anymore.

"We sell some of the women to a man who runs a hog ranch outside Fort Stockton. Ed Kane wears out his women about as fast as the mine owners wear out the men they buy from me. Some of the women run off if they get the chance, and usually wind up dead in the desert. Some of them kill themselves because they can't stand the life. So Kane, like the mine owners, keeps coming back for replacements for the ladies he loses one way or the other.

"What's the matter, Conrad? You don't like the brandy?"

"I'm just not much of a drinking man. I reckon I'm more of a whoremaster, and that being so, I wonder if you'd mind a whole lot if I took a run over to Fort Stockton and paid a visit to the whorehouse this Ed Kane runs."

"You just became a Comanchero and now you want to go on a vacation, is that it?"

"It's not a vacation I want, Camargo. What I want's a woman to scratch the itch between my legs that's been building up for a real long time." Gabe watched Camargo closely to see if the lie he had just told the Comanchero leader had been believed.

"Well, go ahead," Camargo said. "You deserve it, I suppose, considering the way you passed the two tests I set for you with flying colors. But don't dillydally at Kane's place. We'll be riding out to round up some cattle soon—

somebody else's cattle, that is—and you'll be riding with us."

"I'll be looking forward to it. It's been awhile since I've done any rustling and I don't want to get rusty at it," Gabe said. He gave Camargo a haphazard salute, and left the ranch house.

Outside, he stepped into the saddle and rode out, heading for Fort Stockton. The rising sun bored into his back as he rode west, its already furnacelike heat wringing sweat from him that dampened his shirt. He took off his hat as he rode and ran a thumb around its inner band to free it of sweat. Up ahead of him a roadrunner crossed his path, its legs moving swiftly, its tail raised like a signal flag.

He tried not to think of what might be happening to Likes Horses at the hog ranch run by the man named Ed Kane. Hog ranches were not at the top of the list of exclusive bordellos, he knew. Women who worked the hog ranches were usually women who had seen far better days. They were women who, over the years in the life, had drifted downward until they were reduced to servicing soldiers in crude and quick fashion and received little money for each encounter. It was a brutal life, symbolized by the name "hog ranch," and once a woman had sunk to the level of such a place she usually didn't last long. Laudanum, which many such women used to try to dull the sharp edge of their despair, took its often deadly toll.

Several miles and an hour later, Gabe caught his first glimpse of Fort Stockton, which was situated at Comanche Springs on Comanche Creek. Its buildings, which were not fortified, were made of adobe and gleamed white in the sun that was now high in the sky. As Gabe approached the fort, his path was intersected by a stagecoach rumbling past him as it traveled the San Antonio–El Paso stage route. The appearance of the stagecoach reminded him of the reason for the establishment of Fort Stockton back in '59. The primary duty of the infantry stationed at the fort was to protect the stage route but, of late, that duty was being rapidly overshadowed by the army's participation in the Plains Indian wars which, when put down in one place, flared even more hotly in some other spot.

He rode into the fort, past the company quarters buildings, and stopped at the sutler's store, which he knew would be a hotbed of information and gossip to rival that of any livery barn. He dismounted, left his bay tied out front and went inside the store.

"I hear tell," he said to a cadaverous-looking clerk stacking boxes of ammunition, "that there's a hog ranch in the vicinity. I wonder if you could tell me where it is exactly."

"You'll find it a mile north of here. You'll recognize it right off. There's no mistaking Ed Kane's hog ranch. He flies a lady's garter from his flagpole instead of a flag."

"The working women there, how are they, would you say?"

"About the same as at any other whorehouse I've ever been in. A little more sluttish than in some high-toned places, I don't go there for polite company so I've got no complaints."

"Somebody told me there was a real wild Indian woman there," Gabe said with a manufactured leer as he prepared to ask the question of the sutler's clerk that he couldn't risk asking Camargo earlier. "A young Comanche woman. Her name's Likes Horses. Have you—" he couldn't bring himself to say "had her." Instead, he said, "—met her?"

The clerk shook his head. "Can't rightly say if I did or I didn't. I've been with one or two of Kane's Indian sluts, but I was interested in other things at the time besides their names, which didn't make no never mind to me anyhow."

"Well, I thank you for putting me on the right track. I'll be on my way."

Once outside and in the saddle again, Gabe rode away from the fort, heading north. He saw the frayed and faded garter blowing in the breeze at the top of the flagpole that

jutted above a rise before he saw the hog ranch itself.
He rode up the rise and then down it to the establishment itself—a windowless one-story soddy with a stone
chimney that looked as if it were about to tumble to the
ground at any moment, judging by the way the mortar
between its stones had crumbled to allow the structure to
lean precariously.

There was a horse tied out front. A woman with frizzy red
hair was chopping wood on one side of the house and doing
a bad job of it. Gabe rode up to the soddy, dismounted and
wrapped his reins around the hitch rail.

"How do," he said as he rounded the corner of the house.

The woman didn't stop her chopping, nor did she look
up from her task.

"Hot day, isn't it?"

"You come here to do business, mister?"

"I did, yes."

Down came the woman's ax, nearly splitting her foot
instead of the length of timber she had placed on the
chopping block. "It's fifty cents for fifteen minutes. That's
to take it between the legs. In the mouth, for that we charge
two bits extra. You want anything . . . strange—" she gave
Gabe a speculative glance, "you have to work that out with
Ed Kane beforehand."

Gabe decided to plunge right in. "I heard you have a girl
here named Likes Horses. An Indian girl. That true?"

"We've got Indian girls here, yeah, but I never did hear of
that one before. But then Kane, he gives the Indians regular
white folks' names." The woman laughed without merri-
ment. "One of them inside there's named Purity, what do
you think of that?"

Gabe watched as the woman resumed her chopping. Then
he turned and went inside the soddy.

"Welcome, stranger!" boomed a raspy male voice as
Gabe entered the dim interior of the hog ranch. "I'm Ed
Kane and I'm at your service. What'll it be? Whiskey?
Gin?"

Gabe was able to make out a bar at one end of the room that was made of a pine plank supported at either end by two nail kegs. On it were two bottles, one ruddy, one pale—the whiskey and gin Kane had mentioned. The man himself wore no shirt over his long john top, which was soiled and missing its two uppermost buttons. He had a round fleshy face that made Gabe think of the moon from which his pale blue eyes coldly peered.

"Nothing to drink," Gabe told him.

"You're going to dispense with the preliminaries, are you?" Kane declared. "Fine idea. Get right down to the matter at hand, the one that brought you here with your tongue—that is your tongue, isn't it, stranger—hanging out?"

Gabe forced himself to smile as Kane clapped a hand against his thigh and laughed uproariously at the joke he had just made.

"I'll be right with you," he said and came out from behind the bar. He went to a torn curtain that hung nearby and pulled it aside to reveal a cot behind it on which a man and woman were engaged in sexual intercourse. "Time's up, Corporal. You've had your fifteen minutes."

The soldier on top of the woman continued his feeble bucking, his trousers down around his ankles, his face buried in the unkempt hair of the woman lying passively beneath him.

"You heard him," she said and tried to push the soldier away. "You're time's up, Corporal."

"I heard him," the man huffed, "but I know I can come if you'll just give me another minute or two. It never quit on me like this before." His huffing continued until Kane stepped up to the cot, grabbed him by the scruff of the neck and jerked him to his feet.

The corporal stood there, his shaft limp as a wet dishrag, as he tried in vain to argue Kane into giving him more time. But Kane was adamant. He marched the soldier to the door and then through it. When he returned, he was dusting off his hands, and the forlorn corporal, visible through the open door, was cursing as he shamefacedly pulled up and then began buttoning his trousers.

The woman rose from the cot, lowered the chemise she was wearing and sauntered over to where Gabe was standing. "I'll bet yours wouldn't give out on you like that soldier's just did," she cooed.

"Have a seat," Kane said to Gabe after resuming his position behind the bar.

Gabe remained standing. "I hear you've got an Indian woman working here. Her name, somebody told me, is Likes Horses. Pretty little thing. I'd like to buy a bit of her time if she's available."

"We haven't got anybody with a name like that," Kane announced and poured himself a glassful of gin, which he promptly downed with a practiced toss of his head.

"You're sure about that, are you?" Gabe persisted.

"Sure, I'm sure. Whataya think, I don't know the names of my own whores?" More laughter. "Hell, I don't only know their names, I know the size and shape of their you-know-whats. If somebody told you there was a woman here by the name of—What'd you say her name was, the woman you're panting after?"

"Likes Horses."

"Right. Well, whoever told you such a woman was here gave you a bum steer, stranger. But all is not lost, not by a long shot, it's not. There's Lola there. She's ready and raring to go as any fool could plainly see. Look at her! Why, those pretty pouty lips of hers are enough to drive a sane man mad. She's got tits that would put a milch cow to shame. As for what else she's got—you won't be asking for your money back, stranger, once you've rolled around in the hay with little Lola. That there's a money-back guarantee I'm giving you."

Lola simpered. Her hand slid between Gabe's legs.

Gabe's disappointment at the news that Likes Horses was not employed at Kane's hog ranch was almost overpowering. Before he could give serious consideration to his next move Lola had unbuttoned his jeans and taken out his shaft, which was stiffening despite his disappointment and because of her erotic ministrations.

Her manipulation inflamed him. He tried to withdraw but she held him fast, a smile on her face, her tongue flicking provocatively between her lips.

"What's your pleasure, mister?" she whispered.

He wanted to leave. He should leave, he told himself, Likes Horses wasn't there. He would have to search for her elsewhere. He would have to—

Lola's hot hand stroked his throbbing shaft, then dropped down to cup and caress his testicles. "Don't you like me, honey?" she purred. "I could make you like me."

"She's telling you the truth, stranger," Kane declared. "Why don't you give her a tumble? You won't regret it, mark my words."

Lola took Gabe's hand and began to lead him toward the cot hidden behind the curtain. He didn't resist. He had let himself succumb to the raging lust that Lola had aroused in him, and which he now made up his mind to satisfy fully before resuming his search for Likes Horses and the other Comanches.

"Hold it!" Kane called out, raising a beefy hand. "Payment in advance, if you please."

"What are you wanting, honey?" Lola asked, and when he told her, Kane said, "That'll be six bits for fifteen minutes."

Gabe thrust a hand into a pocket of his jeans and came up with the seventy-five cents, which he offered to Lola. She pointed to Kane, so he handed the money to the proprietor of the hog ranch and ducked under the curtain with Lola.

He sat down on the cot, which was covered with a stained sheep blanket and leaned back against the wall.

Lola, wasting no time, dropped to her knees on the floor in front of him and pulled his fly apart. She bent her head and took the head of Gabe's erection into her mouth. He grew even stiffer as he felt her tongue swirl about his shaft, tickling its underside. He reached out and placed his right hand on the back of her head, gently pressing it downward. She offered no resistance, and he watched as inch after stiff inch of his shaft disappeared between her lips. She gagged once when her lips were pressed against his public hair but she quickly recovered. As her head began to bob up and down upon him, Gabe closed his eyes and sighed softly, basking in the intense pleasure she was giving him. Her tongue laved his shaft as she sucked, making him shudder in ecstasy. As she continued to slide her lips up and down along the length of him and continued sucking with a professional skill he had never before encountered in any woman, he felt himself approaching a climax. Passion flamed within him as he opened his eyes and stared down at Lola's rhythmically bobbing head and lips.

He took his hand away from her head and began to move his hips in a series of slow but steady movements—up to meet Lola's descending head and then down as she raised her head and most of his erection came into view. Within seconds their separate rhythms matched perfectly. Gabe could feel the tension building within him, delicious tension that would soon result in a passionate explosion that he knew would rock every inch of his thoroughly aroused body.

Lola raised her head. His shaft slipped out of her mouth. He gripped the back of her head with one hand and took his erection in the other.

"Wait a minute, honey," she gasped as he prodded her lips with the wet head of his shaft, trying to make her take it again and continue what she had been doing. "I got to get my breath. That thing of yours is big enough to choke a horse, not to mention me."

"Take it," he said hoarsely, his words both an order and a plea.

Lola lowered her head and opened her mouth. He sighed

as she took him, all of him, in one swift delightful move. A shiver ran through him as he reveled in the way her tongue was caressing him. And then—she released him again. Before he could protest, she had lowered her head still further and her tongue was on his testicles.

Waves of pleasure, one after the other, washed over him as she laved his scrotum and it tightened in response. Above Lola's head and busy lips, his erection pawed the air. A few crystal droplets of fluid oozed from it. They disappeared as Lola once again took him in her mouth, one of her hands gripping his stone-stiff shaft at its base while the other caressed his testicles.

He groaned. Tossed his head from side to side. Raised his hips . . .

He was ready to erupt.

Lola seemed to sense that fact. Her lips tightened on him. The gurgling sounds she was making as she continued sucking and simultaneously stroking his shaft grew louder.

He seized her head with both hands. He held it firmly in place as he thrust himself down her throat and exploded. Surge after surge of thrilling sensations caused him to cry out. His entire body began to spasm just as his shaft was doing inside Lola's mouth. Looking down at her as he continued to discharge in her mouth, he saw her working frantically as she swallowed all he had to give her.

Feeling completely drained, he released his hold on Lola's head.

She pulled away from him. Wiping her lips with the back of her hand, she winked at him. "I bet you feel like you could lick your weight in butterflies about now, am I right or am I wrong?"

"Honey, you are as right as rain and that's a true fact," Gabe murmured, leaning his head back against the wall, his eyes closed.

"It's still stiff," Lola marveled.

He felt her take him in her hand and gently stroke him, the wetness she had left on his shaft making sucking sounds

as she did so. Her stroking became faster. And then still
faster. She watched his face. When his eyes squeezed shut
and his body tensed her stroking reached a furious pace.

He sprayed her chemise and her hand when he came a
second time. He took a deep breath and let it out. He opened
his eyes. He reached out and caressed Lola's cheek. "Honey, you are a wonder and a half."

Lola smiled. "Practice makes perfect."

"Time's up!" bellowed Kane from beyond the curtain.

Gabe was up on his feet and tucking himself into his jeans
when Kane pulled the curtain aside and announced, "Lola,
I've got two at a time for you. Both boys are from Fort
Stockton and both are willing to pay extra to get in your
front and back doors at the same time. Clear out, stranger,"
Kane concluded, gesturing toward Gabe.

Buttoning his fly, Gabe brushed past Kane and the two
eager-eyed sergeants standing directly behind him and made
his way out of the hog ranch. He boarded his bay and rode
out, the satisfaction he had obtained with Lola—the sense of
physical release—fast fading as his thoughts turned again to
Likes Horses and the other Comanches who had been sold
by Carmargo. He shouldn't have leaped to the conclusion that
Likes Horses would be at that hog ranch back there, he
told himself. Carmargo never said that's where she was and
Gabe couldn't come right out and ask him what he'd done
with her. Not without blowing the game, he couldn't.

Where the hell is she? he wondered as he rode back toward
the Comanchero headquarters. It was a question he wished
he could ask Camargo without arousing suspicion. Maybe,
he thought, he could ask some more questions about who
Camargo's customers are and for what purposes they buy
the Comanche captives. Maybe that way he could get a hint
of what's happened to Likes Horses.

But how many questions could he ask, he wondered,
before Camargo got the idea that he didn't come to his
place just to join his gang of Comancheros. Gabe turned
the problem facing him over and over in his mind as he

journeyed east. He had found no satisfactory solution to it by the time he arrived at his destination.

He was just emerging from the canyon when he heard a rifle shot fired by whoever was standing guard on the mesa above him. He looked up but could not see the rifleman. He could, however, hear the sound of horses coming from behind him. He estimated that he was hearing the sounds made by at least four horses heading in his direction. His hand dropped to the butt of his revolver as he sat his saddle waiting to see who was approaching at such a fast and furious pace.

Within seconds, he had his answer. Apaches. He tensed when he saw the first of them emerge from the canyon. He was prepared to shoot if he recognized any of them as members of Cha-lipun's band. He scanned the faces of the six riders as they all came into view and was vastly relieved to find that he recognized none of them. But that didn't mean, he knew very well, that he was out of the woods as far as the Indians were concerned. It could be that one or more of them had recognized him. If they had, they gave no outward sign of having done so, which brought him a sweet sense of relief. He took his hand from his gun and rode toward the ranch house behind the Apaches.

When they stopped in front of the ranch house and dismounted, he rode around them, got out of the saddle and, leaving his horse ground-hitched, went inside.

He found Camargo heading for the front door, a cigar in his mouth, smoke swirling around him.

"We've got visitors," Gabe told him.

"So I see."

He followed Camargo out of the house and stood to one side as the Comanchero leader and the Apaches exchanged greetings.

After several minutes had passed, one of the Apaches turned and pointed to the mouth of the canyon where a wagon had just driven into sight. In the back of the wagon, packed tightly together, were nine men, and a woman to whom two children—a boy of about ten and a girl about half that age—clung, their faces buried in her skirt. All of them were Paiute Indians. The driver of the wagon, an Apache, pulled up in front of the house and halted.

The apparent leader of the band of Apaches pointed to the people in the wagon and told Camargo, "Strong men. Young woman. Children strong too. Grow up soon. How much you pay us for them?"

"Five cases of whiskey for the men," Camargo said. "Half a case for the woman."

"How much you give us for the children?"

"Colchinay, I've told you this before," Camargo said in the weary voice of a teacher talking to a slow-learning pupil, "I have no use for children. I can't sell them because nobody wants them. They are useless to me. You can keep them."

"What Colchinay do with Paiute children? He does not need them."

Camargo gave an eloquent shrug and turned his hands out, palms up, in a gesture of helplessness.

"Colchinay want ten cases whiskey for them." He gestured to the wagonload of Paiute prisoners.

Camargo laughed heartily and shook his head. "Colchinay," he said mockingly, "is a highway robber. I'm offering five and a half cases and that's my final offer. Take it or leave it."

"Eight cases."

Camargo turned to reenter the ranch house.

Colchinay quickly reached out and put a hand on his arm to prevent him from doing so.

Camargo turned, looked down at the brown hand on his white shirt and shook it off.

"We take five and a half cases whiskey," Colchinay said with flint in his voice and murder in his eyes.

Camargo cupped his hands around his mouth and shouted, "Sanchez! Vickers!"

Both men promptly emerged from the bunkhouse and hurried over to where their leader stood waiting for them.

"Sanchez, take these Indians to the barn," Camargo ordered. "Then stand guard over them. Vickers, give Colchinay five and a half cases of whiskey."

Vickers headed for one of the outbuildings as Sanchez, his gun drawn, began to herd the Paiute captives toward the barn.

Colchinay stepped forward and seized by their hair both of the children who were clinging to the woman. As he tried to pull them away from her she began to scream and fight frantically to keep them with her. Colchinay struck her in the face with a fisted hand but the savage blow neither stopped her screaming nor her struggle to keep the children with her.

One of the other Apaches stepped up behind the woman and put his brawny arms around her. He pulled her in one direction while Colchinay, still gripping the two children by their hair, pulled them in the opposite direction.

"No!" the woman screeched at the top of her voice as she was forcibly separated from the boy and girl. "Give me back my children!" she screamed, her arms reaching out to them as they too began to scream and struggle in vain to free themselves from Colchinay.

Her screams could still be heard once she was imprisoned within the barn with the rest of the captives. The children's screams echoed hers.

Vickers had returned and finished loading the whiskey in the wagon bed when Colchinay turned the screaming girl over to a taciturn Apache standing nearby and then drew his knife.

As if his act had been a signal, the other Apache holding the little girl also drew his knife. Both men promptly slit the throats of the two children from ear to ear and let their bloody bodies fall to the ground in front of Camargo.

Then they boarded their horses and moved out, the wagon loaded with whiskey following behind them.

"Vickers," Camargo said, his mouth twisting in distaste, "clean up that mess those redskins left behind."

After Camargo had returned to the house, Gabe stood watching as Vickers, gripping the corpses of the two children by their ankles, dragged them around the side of the bunkhouse and out of sight.

That night Gabe attended the meeting Camargo had called to discuss the planned theft of the cattle herd Camargo had mentioned earlier. Also present were Sanchez and Vickers. Smoke filled the room as they sat around an oak table and made their plans. Camargo plotted their plan of attack with the stub of a pencil on the back of an old bill of lading.

"Vickers," he said, making an X on one side of the paper beneath his hand, "you and the men with you will ride in on the herd from this direction. Sanchez, you and your riders will come down on the herd from the hills to the east." Camargo wet the point of his pencil and made another X near the top of the paper. "You'll both drive them north past Deep Creek here"—another X—"and them down into the draw at Devil's Gulch."

"Then what?" Vickers asked as he vigorously picked his teeth with a broken fingernail.

"We'll drive them east after we leave the gulch and on up into the high country. Conrad, you and Sanchez will stand guard over them until we've disposed of them. There's an old line-rider's shack up there where we're taking them. It's been abandoned for years now ever since the Folsom ranch went bankrupt. We keep it stocked with supplies for occasions such as this."

"You bring the cattle buyers up there to the high country to look over the stock, do you?" Gabe asked.

"No," Camargo answered, shaking his head. "We don't want anybody knowing where we hide the cattle we steal. After a few days you and Sanchez will drive them down here to the ranch. Then I'll get the word out to potential buyers and we'll unload them."

"I expect there'll be men patrolling the herd's bed ground when we get there," Gabe commented.

"A few, yes," Camargo said as he stubbed out the cigar he had been smoking and promptly proceeded to clip the end off another one and then light it.

"We'll stop their clocks before they even know we're in the vicinity," Vickers stated bluntly.

"You mean—" Gabe began.

But Vickers interrupted him. "We'll kill them."

When Gabe glanced at Camargo, the Comanchero leader said, "Why do you look so pained, my friend? We cannot leave witnesses to our thieving behind, now can we?"

"When exactly do you intend to make this raid?" Gabe asked.

Before Camargo could answer, the sound of a rifle shot shattered the silence of the night.

"Somebody's coming," Sanchez muttered, going for his gun as he got to his feet and went to the door.

"Can you see who it is?" Camargo asked.

Sanchez didn't reply for a moment as he opened the door and peered out into the darkness, his gun unholstered and in his hand. "It's Mr. Carstairs."

"I'll break out the booze," Camargo announced, rising and going to a cabinet from which he extracted a bottle of brandy.

"Evening, Mr. Carstairs," Sanchez said into the darkness beyond the door.

Gabe heard the nicker of a horse and then the sound of boots hitting the ground.

"Evening, Sanchez. Is Camargo in?"

"Yes, sir, he's here."

Sanchez stepped aside and a big burly man strode into the room, his sunburst spurs jingling and his boot heels pounding the planks of the board floor.

"Welcome, Sid," Camargo said and filled a glass with brandy. He handed it to his guest, who took it and then sat down at the table. "What can I do for you this time, Sid?" Camargo asked, sitting down opposite the man.

"I want a woman," Carstairs blurted out.

"You want a woman?" Camargo grinned the grin of a snake. "Don't we all? Ah, yes, don't we all?"

"I'll pay top dollar for the right woman," Carstairs said and drank most of his brandy. "The one I bought from you a few months ago, she up and ran off on me."

"You couldn't find her?"

"I didn't want to wear out a good horse hunting for her. I figured it'd be easier to buy me a new one. A fresh one. Fucking the one I had wasn't much fun or frolic there toward the end. All she did was cry. I couldn't get her to stop no matter how hard I hit her. I tell you, that kind of female foolishness takes the starch out of a man's pecker faster than snow melts in the halls of hell."

"I've got a woman out in the barn right this minute as it happens," Camargo declared. "Got her today. She's young. A Paiute. Do you want to take a look at her?"

Carstairs nodded and drained the brandy in his glass.

As Camargo refilled his guest's glass, he said, "Vickers, go get the woman and bring her in here."

Vickers got to his feet and lumbered out of the room.

When he returned a few minutes later, he had with him the young Paiute woman, who stood with her head lowered, her shoulders slumping, her eyes dull.

Camargo rose and went over to her. He put out a hand and, gripping her chin, tilted her head upward. "Not bad looking, is she?" he asked, directing his question to Carstairs, who was studying the woman as he thoughtfully stroked his chin. "She's got quite a figure too." He reached out with his free hand and ripped the woman's buckskin dress so that her breasts were bared.

Carstairs' eyes narrowed. He licked his lips.

The woman stood without moving, seemingly unmindful of Camargo's hand on her chin or her partial nudity. She stared without expression at the wall facing her.

Carstairs rose and moved toward her like a man sleep-walking. He stopped directly in front of her and began to fondle her breasts. The woman whimpered faintly but she did not attempt to withdraw. Carstairs' hand slid downward through the rent in her dress.

"How much?" he asked Camargo, his voice unsteady.

The two men proceeded to haggle over the price for the Paiute woman while she simply stood and let Carstairs' rough hands have their way with her. A price was finally agreed upon and the two men, when Carstairs' money was in Camargo's pocket, shook hands.

"You've got yourself a prize," Camargo declared expansively, indicating the woman. "She'll cure whatever ails you."

"She's not bad," Carstairs grudgingly admitted, "but I have to tell you I'd been hoping for something better ever since I laid eyes on that woman you sold to Dade Farley the other day."

"Which woman was that?" Camargo asked.

"Farley calls her Charlotte, but at first she wouldn't answer to it, not until Farley took a switch to her. She said her name was Likes Horses."

Gabe, at the sound of the name, almost shot up out of his chair. He forced himself to remain calm.

"She told Farley she wouldn't answer to no other name but her own. But then, like I said, Farley took a switch to her and she'd answer him now if he called her Shit."

"How's Farley doing these days?" Camargo asked idly as he poured himself some brandy.

"He's expanding. He's building himself a bigger barn and adding more steers to his herd, which is already about the biggest one west of here. He's talking about setting up a logging operation to make money out of all that timber he's got on his land. He claims that big old forest of cedar trees is going to make him a rich man."

Carstairs placed a ham like hand on the Paiute woman's upper arm. "We'll be leaving you now, Camargo."

"Enjoy yourself, my friend. Enjoy *her*."

Carstairs glanced over his shoulder as he walked the woman he had just purchased toward the door. "I intend to do that very thing just as soon as I get her home. Good night all."

When Carstairs had gone, Gabe leaned back in his chair and, with his thoughts racing, said as casually as he could, "It would seem there are all sorts of ways for a man to make money these days."

Camargo gave him a quizzical glance.

"This fellow that Carstairs just mentioned—Farley?"

"Dade Farley."

"Right. He sounds all set to turn a bunch of useless trees into a cash crop. I wonder where he's fixing to sell them. Is there a sawmill around these parts somewhere?"

"He no doubt intends to haul them up to San Antonio. His ranch isn't more than ten, twelve miles southwest of there."

Gabe forced himself to yawn, although he was not the least bit sleepy. "Well, I reckon I'll turn in and get me some shut-eye."

"We'll be ready to ride out first thing in the morning," Camargo reminded him just before Gabe stepped out into the night, excitement surging within him now that he finally knew where to find Likes Horses.

CHAPTER SEVEN

Gabe headed for the corral, eager to be on his way to find Like Horses and return her to her grandfather. When he reached it, he swung open the corral's gate and went inside to where his bay and a black were devouring the last of a bale of hay he had thrown into the corral earlier in the day.

He took his gear down from one of the corral's poles and proceeded to get his horse ready to ride. He was tightening his cinch strap when an idea occurred to him. He stopped what he was doing and stood there, a smile slowly spreading across his face. He finished securing his cinch strap, then let his bay out of the corral. He left it standing ground-hitched midway between the corral and the barn that loomed ahead of him in the dark night.

Perfect, he thought. No moon. Only a star or two's able to poke through the cloud cover. A perfect night for the plan he had in mind. He moved forward stealthily, careful not to make any noise, gingerly planting one foot in front of the other after first surveying the ground carefully, heading toward the dim figure leaning against the barn door. As he came closer to the man, he could make out his face. Cuchillo. The Indian who rode with the Comancheros. The sight of the man angered him. What kind of man would turn on his own as Cuchillo had done? The thought of an Indian helping to enslave his own kind for profit made him hate the sight of the Apache.

He halted and looked around. There was no one in sight. The only sounds audible in the darkness were those of an owl hooting mournfully in a distant tree. Gabe moved forward, one cautious step at a time.

When only steps separated him from the Indian, who was wearing a six-gun on his hip and a knife on his belt, Gabe eased to one side so that he could come in on Cuchillo's blind side as the man stared off toward the mouth of the canyon in the distance.

Cuchillo reached up to scratch his head. He shifted his weight from one foot to the other and then abruptly turned in Gabe's direction.

"Nice night," Gabe said to him as he strode forward, trying to appear nonchalant.

Cuchillo didn't respond at first. Then he asked, "What the hell are you doing prowling around out here?"

"Prowling? Who's prowling? All I'm doing, partner, is trying to tire myself out so I can get some sleep. I hit my bunk a little while ago but I couldn't sleep a wink, so I came out here to walk around awhile before I try again to get some shut-eye."

Cuchillo said nothing. He merely eyed Gabe impassively.

"You riding with us tomorrow?" Gabe asked, watching for an opportunity to take the man.

Cuchillo nodded, then swiftly turned away from Gabe at the sound of something in the night, which turned out to be a foraging muskrat. Before he could turn back again, Gabe wrapped his right arm around the man's throat from behind and pressed down hard on the side of the man's neck with his left thumb. Cuchillo struggled to free himself. He seized Gabe's restraining arm with both hands and pulled on it.

But Gabe's arm didn't give so much as a fraction of an inch. He pressed harder with his thumb, gouging the Apache's throat.

Cuchillo began to gag. Then, suddenly, his grip on Gabe's arm loosened. A moment later, his hands fell away to hang limply by his sides as his entire body went limp.

Gabe removed his thumb from the man's neck, pleased that the pressure of his thumb had finally rendered the Indian unconscious. He let the man fall to the ground in a senseless heap. Stepping over him, he swung open the barn door and found himself confronting an almost total darkness in which no sound could be heard.

"Hey!" he said into the darkness. "I'm here to get you fellows out of here."

No response.

He turned and gave the barn door a shove to open it wider. As he did so, a figure suddenly materialized out of the darkness, seized Gabe by the throat and began to throttle him. Gabe kneed the man in the groin, breaking his hold.

"Dammit to hell!" he muttered through his clenched teeth, "I'm here to help you and you try to kill me!"

In the thin light from the partially starred sky outside, Gabe, as his eyes became accustomed to the gloom, was able to make out the Paiutes standing together on one side of the ladder that led to the hay loft.

"Come on," he said to them and gestured toward the open door in case they didn't understand him. "We're getting out of here. Come *on!*"

The imprisoned men looked at one another. Then they looked at Gabe and finally at the open door.

Gabe gestured toward it again, his motions frantic. But it was not until he ran forward, took one of the Paiutes by the arm and rushed him outside that the other men followed, their pace gradually quickening.

"To the corral," he muttered just loud enough for them

to hear him. He pointed to it. "There are horses there. Take what you need. Get out of here!"

"Why you do this?" one of the Paiutes asked him.

"Never mind about that now. It's too long a story and I don't have time to tell it to you. Just go, will you, while the going's good? If you fellas don't get a move on that guard lying there's liable to wake up and give the alarm, and then you'll find yourselves right back in the fix I'm trying my damnedest to get you all out of."

The Paiutes began to move toward the corral, a few of them giving Gabe suspicious glances over their shoulders as they did so.

"Walk your horses away from the canyon," he ordered the Paiutes. "They've got a guard posted up there on the mesa. Make sure he doesn't see you. Head for those hills back there. But don't make any noise till you're over the first rise. Then ride like the wind."

He climbed aboard his bay as the Paiutes began to lope silently toward the corral. He sat his saddle and watched as each man led a horse from it and then moved in the direction of the nearby hills. He returned the wave one of the men gave him and then, when the last of the Indians had topped the rise and dropped out of sight, he did as they had done. He walked his horse away from the canyon. When he was sure that he was far enough away so that he could not be heard, he spurred the bay and went galloping northwest.

He remained on the trail for what he estimated was a good three hours, judging by the position of the polestar, before he drew rein and dismounted. He spread his tarp and blanket and placed his gun on the ground as he lay down. Then he pulled off his boots, hat and gun belt. He wrapped himself in his blanket and soon was asleep.

When he awoke the sun was above the horizon and in the distance a rooster was crowing. He sat up, shook out his boots and then pulled them on. He holstered his revolver, clapped his hat on his head and tied his tarp and blanket behind the cantle of his saddle. He climbed aboard his bay and rode in the direction from which the sound made by the rooster had come. When he reached a bluff above a small soddy he knew he was not looking at the Farley homestead. This one was too small and hardscrabble-looking and there was no cedar forest anywhere near it.

He rode down from the bluff and brought his horse to a halt in front of the house. He called out a hello and, in response, the door swung open on its leather hinges and a grizzled old man who looked to be on the far side of seventy emerged from the dwelling.

"Good day to you," Gabe greeted the man. "I'm looking for the Farley place. I was told it was about ten miles or so southwest of San Antonio. Is it near here, by any chance?"

"That depends on what you mean by near," the old man answered. "That crick yonder"—he pointed to it—"now I'd call that near. But the Farley place? No, I wouldn't call *that* near. No way would I."

A smile spread across Gabe's face as he decided he would have to be more precise in the way he phrased his next questions if he were to obtain satisfactory—specific—answers to them.

"How many miles from here is the Farley place and which way do I to get to it?"

"It's five miles, maybe a mite more, as the crow flies, though you clearly ain't no kind of crow. It's off that way." The man jerked a thumb over his shoulder.

"I'm much obliged for the information." He rode away, heading in the direction the old man had indicated, and before the sun had reached its meridian he spotted a forest of cedar trees up ahead of him. To the right of the forest and about five hundred yards away from it was a two-story frame house painted white with black shutters on all of its windows. It had several gables and an L-shaped front porch. Zinnias grew in front of the house and there were lace curtains on the windows. Behind the house was a small red barn, and next to it another larger barn was under construction, although no one was working on it at the moment. Cattle meandered through a lush pasture a half mile from the house and barns.

Gabe rode up to the house, dismounted, climbed up on the porch and knocked on the front door. Out of the corner of his eye he saw the curtain covering the window on his left move slightly. A moment later the door opened and he found himself facing a tall woman whose slender frame consisted more of bone than flesh. Her pale face was gaunt. Her black hair was drawn back in a bun at the nape of her neck. Her gray eyes glittered. Gabe estimated her age at no more than thirty, but to him she looked more like forty because of the severity of her facial expression and the somber and unadorned black bombazine dress she wore.

"Good morning, ma'am," he said, touching the brim of his hat to her. "My name's Gabe Conrad. I stopped by to talk to Mr. Dade Farley."

"My husband is not at home, Mr. Conrad," she said in an even tone, each word she uttered a kind of sharp exclamation.

"I'm sorry to hear that. I've come a long way to talk to him."

"About business?"

Gabe hesitated a brief moment and then answered, "Yes, about business, Mrs. Farley." Well, he thought, that's the truth. In a loose manner of speaking.

"Please come in. You're welcome to wait for him inside out of the sun. I expect him shortly. He went to Abilene on business."

Gabe doffed his hat and followed Mrs. Farley into the relatively cool interior of the house, which he found was expensively and tastefully furnished. He scanned the place as he followed Mrs. Farley into a parlor that contained heavy pieces of claw-footed furniture, which were all upholstered in black leather.

"You mentioned that you've come a long way to see my husband, Mr. Conrad," Mrs. Farley said, standing in front of a marble fireplace with her hands folded in front of her. "Have you had dinner?"

"No, ma'am, I've not as a matter of fact. The last meal I had was supper last night."

"Then you must be hungry. I'll get you something to eat. If you'll excuse me."

"I don't want to put you to any trouble, Mrs. Farley, but I sure do appreciate your hospitality."

"My husband would expect nothing less of me, Mr. Conrad."

When Mrs. Farley had left the room, Gabe went to the archway at the other end of the room and peered into the dining room. Empty. He retraced his steps and went out into the entrance hall. From there he could see into the kitchen at the far end of the hall, but he saw no sign of Likes Horses in the room, nor could he hear voices coming from it.

Mrs. Farley appeared in the kitchen doorway, a large platter in her hands, and halted when she saw Gabe. "Is something amiss, Mr. Conrad?"

"No, ma'am. I was—I was just looking around your lovely home. It's real nice. And you keep it up just fine."

"My husband likes a well-kept home," Mrs. Farley said as she walked down the hall and turned right into the dining room, which contained a massive mahogany table and six ornately carved chairs as well as a sideboard and a china cabinet. The room's floor-to-ceiling windows were covered in lace and bordered by red velvet drapes.

"Please sit down, Mr. Conrad." When he did, Mrs. Farley placed the platter on the table. It held slices of cold ham, roast beef, and lamb. She left the room and returned with a basketful of bread, a bread knife, a pot of mustard and a glass bowl containing catsup, all of which she placed on the table in front of Gabe.

"Would you like some coffee? Tea perhaps?"

"Coffee would be fine."

He was making himself a roast beef sandwich when she returned with a tray on which rested a coffeepot, a pitcher, a sugar bowl, and two porcelain cups and saucers that bore painted garlands of roses on their rims.

She placed the tray on the table and sat down opposite him. "Milk, Mr. Conrad? Sugar?"

"I take it black."

She filled a cup and handed it to him.

"Strong," he said when he had tasted it. "Just the way I like it." He watched her pour a cup of coffee for herself as he took a big bite out of his sandwich. She poured milk and spooned sugar into her cup.

"What time did you say your husband would be home?"

"I didn't mention any particular time, as I recall. But I did say I expect him soon."

"He's got himself a thriving place here. I saw the new barn he's building. And somebody told me he's fixing to cut down that cedar forest yonder and haul the logs up to San Antonio to sell."

"Oh, my husband is a most enterprising man, Mr. Conrad. He lets no grass grow under his feet, so to speak. He's been quite successful at every endeavor he has turned his hand to. Many people envy him his success."

"I can understand that," Gabe said and took another bite of his sandwich.

"Many people think Dade is a happy man," Mrs. Farley said, not looking at Gabe as she sipped her coffee.

He caught—or thought he did—the dark implication in her seemingly offhand remark. "You're saying—correct me if I'm wrong—that your husband's not a happy man."

"That's correct. He isn't. If he were a happy man he would be content to stay at home more with his wife of lo, these nine long years. He wouldn't gamble the way he does. My husband has lost three thousand dollars so far this year in the casinos in San Antonio, Mr. Conrad. Such a loss does not, however, deter him. He continues to gamble. Just as he continues to drink and tomcat his way through the world with any willing woman without giving a moment's thought to appearances or the feelings of anyone but himself."

Deep water, Gabe thought. I'm getting into deep water here. Deep and troubled water.

"Do my remarks surprise you, Mr. Conrad?" Without waiting for a reply to her question, Mrs. Farley continued. "I have always been a rather outspoken person. In addition, what I have said about my husband betrays no confidences, nor does it let any cat out of the bag. My husband's carousing—his gambling, drinking and womanizing—is well known within the borders of this state, and perhaps beyond them, for all I know. I'm sure you've heard the talk that is bandied about concerning him."

"Well, no, ma'am, I've not," Gabe said, finishing the last of his sandwich. "But if you say it's so, I reckon it is."

"Have no doubt about it, Mr. Conrad. Would you like another sandwich?"

"No, thank you, ma'am, I've had sufficient."

"Another cup of coffee then." Mrs. Farley poured one for him. "I have some little cakes in the kitchen—"

Gabe shook his head and held up a hand. "I'm fine, thanks. The roast beef was delicious. So was the bread. It's been quite a spell since I've had such good home-baked bread."

"I busy myself these days at such tasks as baking bread and those little cakes I mentioned. One must keep one's self busy, mustn't one? Especially when one has a drunken philandering gambler for a husband. Such harmless tasks take one's mind off troubles, I assure you. What about some wine, Mr. Conrad?"

"I—"

Gabe fell silent as Mrs. Farley went to the sideboard, opened one of its doors and took out a bottle of sherry and two crystal glasses. She carried them back to the table and filled the glasses. She handed one to Gabe and then raised her own. "A toast," she proposed, "to happy days." She drank. Gabe's glass remained untouched. "You don't like sherry, Mr. Conrad?"

"I'm not what you could call a drinking man, Mrs. Farley."

"A blessing, Mr. Conrad. Would that I could say the same about Dade." She refilled her glass and then promptly emptied it. "But, alas, I cannot."

Gabe noticed the wetness that was making her gray eyes glitter even more brightly than usual as she twirled the sherry bottle between her hands. He pretended not to notice when she hiccupped.

By the time she had drained her third glass of sherry, her words were beginning to become slightly slurred. "I didn't always wear black, Mr. Conrad," she declared without preamble. "But black becomes me, I think, as it does any woman in mourning. Oh, you needn't look so startled. Yes, I am indeed in mourning. I mourn for what once was between Dade and me, the fine and wonderful thing that died so many years ago of neglect and apathy.

"I did not always look like this or dress like this or talk this way to strangers. As to that last point—" another hiccup, "one must talk to someone about the pain one feels, mustn't one? And if there are no lovers or friends to talk to, then strangers will have to do." She gave a little laugh as if she had made a quite enjoyable joke and added, "Let me show you something."

Gabe rose when she did but she gestured to indicate that he was to resume his seat. She went into the parlor and returned with a photograph framed under glass. She held it up in front of her with both hands so that it was facing Gabe. "Do you recognize me?"

Gabe almost didn't. The woman in the photograph looked years younger than Mrs. Farley but, upon close inspection, an observer would discover that it was indeed her. In the photograph, her hair was put up, but not in the severe bun she now wore. It was piled high upon her head in wave after raven wave and held in place by a jeweled comb. Her eyes laughed and her lips smiled. Her entire expression was one of unalloyed joy as she gazed longingly and lovingly at the man standing in striped coat and banded straw hat by her side, her arm linked in his. She was wearing a white dress and a long string of seed pearls that contrasted sharply with the color of her hair. On her feet were a dainty pair of white satin slippers so unlike the stiff high-button shoes she was wearing now.

"The man in the picture," she said dully, "is my husband."

Dade Farley, as he appeared in the photograph, was a well-built man with a boyish grin and a shock of brown hair that fell down over his broad forehead. Handsome, Gabe decided. But there was an emptiness in his eyes that was disturbing.

"This was taken eight years ago," Mrs. Farley declared. "On the first anniversary of our marriage. We were still happy then, but there was talk about Dade's exploits even in those early days. I paid no heed. I was aware that many people gossiped about others who had succeeded where they had failed or done poorly. I chose to believe the stories of Dade's infidelities were just that—stories. Lies. By the time another year had passed I knew they were more than that. Dade denied them and oh, how desperately I wanted to believe his denials. Then, as more time passed, I made myself believe him when, instead of bothering to deny his extramarital affairs and his habitual gambling and drinking, he promised me faithfully that he would abandon his dissolute way of life, turn over a new leaf and live decently and love only me."

Mrs. Farley placed the photograph facedown on the table. She picked up the sherry bottle and refilled her empty glass. She took a deep breath and then emptied the glass. She went to the window and stared out, her back to Gabe, her voice, when it came again, harsh.

"Dade broke every promise he ever made to me, Mr. Conrad. In the process he broke my heart. Time and time again. Do you know what it is to want to believe someone so desperately and then to find out that that someone has

repeatedly lied to you? It closes all your doors, Mr. Conrad.
You learn to remain hidden behind them. You talk less. You
begin to forget how to laugh. You no longer wear yellow
and red and green dresses. You put your jewels away and
never look at them again. You turn from a young woman
wildly in love into a cold bloodless bitch!"

At the word "bitch," Mrs. Farley turned from the window
to face Gabe. "It's true, Mr. Conrad. Sometimes my husband tries to—take me. I refuse him. I sleep—have slept for
years—in what was to have been the nursery." She laughed,
a merciless sound like that of glass shattering.

"Mrs. Farley, I'm sorry for your trouble. . . . "

She seemed not to have heard Gabe. She wandered away
from the window, her empty sherry glass upended in her
hand. Drops of wine fell from it to stain her skirt. She
returned to the table and sat down. She seemed only then
to become aware of the glass in her hand. She put it down
on the table and said, "Dade has recently taken up with an
Indian woman, Mr. Conrad."

Gabe stiffened as he waited for her to go on.

"An Indian woman he *bought*!" she exclaimed. "He told
me I needed help in the house. He told me I needed a servant. He brought that heathen into my home and installed
her in the spare room upstairs. Perhaps he thinks I do not
hear him during the nights when he visits her and they—
they—" She looked away when the words wouldn't come.
"He took her with him to Abilene." She turned her head and
gave Gabe a ghastly smile. "He has become quite enamored
of her, it seems. Isn't that remarkable?"

Gabe didn't know what to say as anger at Dade Farley
and a terrible pity for the man's wife engulfed him.

"I have thoughts, Mr. Conrad," Mrs. Farley continued.
"I have frightening thoughts of guns and knives and potent
poisons. Sometimes, when I am, as is so often the case,
alone here, I let myself imagine that I really have murdered
my husband and I feel, while the fantasy lives, at peace.
Do you find me hateful, Mr. Conrad?"

"If what you've been telling me is all true, I think you've had a hard row to hoe in life, Mrs. Farley."

She nodded and returned to the window, where she stood twisting her hands as if she were washing them.

"Even religion doesn't help," she said. "Religion," she snorted disdainfully. "Nothing but empty words to speak and silly songs to sing on Sunday. Nothing helps. Nothing at all. Because, you see, underneath it all and despite everything I've just said, I still love Dade as much as I did on the day we were married, heaven help me. That, Mr. Conrad, is the cruelest joke of all that life has played on me."

When the tears came then, Gabe didn't hesitate. He got up from the table and went to Mrs. Farley. He took her by the shoulders and turned her away from the window. He held her as she buried her face against his broad chest and sobbed, her body shuddering violently.

"Maybe there's one small thing I can do that might help you some," he told her.

For a moment her sobbing stopped, but then it began again almost immediately.

"The reason I've come here, Mrs. Farley, is to take the Indian woman you mentioned away from here."

She looked up at him. "You mean Charlotte?"

"That's not her name."

"That's what Dade calls her. He told me that was her name."

"It's not. Her name is Likes Horses and she happens to be a friend of mine."

Mrs. Farley, her eyes glistening with tears, said in a voice so soft it was almost inaudible, "She is most fortunate in having a friend like you. I know because of the kindness you have shown me here today. The kindness for which, I must tell you, I am most grateful."

Mrs. Farley withdrew from Gabe's embrace. She patted her hair, a nervous gesture, looked around the dining room as if in search of something, and then went to the table. "I'll clear up," she said and began to do so.

Gabe was seated in the parlor some time later awaiting her return when he heard the jingle of harnesses outside. He got up and went to the window. Through the gauzy film of the lace curtain covering it, he saw a wagon pull up in front of the house. His heart leaped at the sight of Likes Horses seated next to the driver of the wagon who was, although not exactly the same in physical appearance as the man in the photograph Mrs. Farley had earlier displayed, unmistakably Dade Farley.

His face was puffy now and there were ragged red veins visible on his nose. The lock of brown hair still fell forward on his forehead, but now there was a faint touch of gray in it. But he moved easily and there was an aura of physical strength about the man. He was wearing a checkered vest under his sack coat, nankeen trousers and a dusty brown derby.

He offered his hand to Likes Horses, but she ignored it and stepped down from the carriage without his aid. Farley gestured and she responded by stepping up on the porch and reaching for the doorknob.

Gabe hurried out of the parlor. He was standing in the entrance hall when the door opened and Likes Horses, her eyes widening and her mouth opening in surprise at the unexpected sight of him, stepped inside the house.

She let out a little cry and ran to him. Her arms went around him and she hugged him so tightly he had trouble getting his breath.

"Well, well, what have we here?" Farley said as he entered the house behind Likes Horses.

"We have a guest who has come to do business with you, Dade," Mrs. Farley said as she came down the hall from the kitchen toward the trio standing in the entrance hall. "This gentleman's name is Gabe Conrad. Mr. Conrad, my husband, Dade Farley."

"Always glad to meet a fellow businessman, Mr. Conrad," Farley said, offering his hand.

When Gabe didn't shake it, Farley frowned and withdrew

it. "What can I do for you, Mr. Conrad?"

"I've come to collect the lady," Gabe answered.

Farley's gaze shifted to his wife and then back to Gabe. "I say you are insulting, sir. You've come to collect my wife?"

"Sorry," Gabe said. "I didn't make myself clear. I'm here to take Likes Horses away with me."

"You're here to—" Farley frowned again. Then his frown dissolved and he began to giggle. "Forgive me for my confusion of a moment ago. But you did say 'lady,' did you not, Mr. Conrad?"

"That's right."

"I would hardly call Charlotte a lady."

"I'm willing to pay you what you paid Miguel Camargo for her," Gabe said, fighting to control his temper.

"My goodness, this is something of a surprise. So, Mr. Conrad, is your straightforward—I might even say blunt—manner of doing business."

"I don't want to waste time, Farley. How much did you pay Camargo for Likes Horses?"

"That, sir, is none of your business. It also happens to be irrelevant since the lady, as you so amusingly choose to call her, is not for sale."

Likes Horses, who had been smiling broadly from the moment she first saw Gabe, grew somber, her smile vanishing completely.

"Dade," Mrs. Farley said, "It is quite alright with me if you dispose of Char—Likes Horses. I really have no need of a servant. I am quite capable of taking care of our home myself and—"

"Silence!" Farley snapped.

She's bound and determined to keep up her playacting, Gabe thought with a sidelong glance in Mrs. Farley's direction. She's one sorry lady, that's for sure. Turning his attention to Farley again, he said, "Let me put it to you this way. I either pay you the price you paid Camargo for Likes Horses or I take her away from here without paying you one red cent. Now, what's your pleasure, Farley?"

Farley's gaze dropped to the gun on Gabe's hip. "So that's how the land lies, is it?" He raised his eyes to stare thoughtfully at Gabe. "May I make so bold as to ask what your interest in *the lady*"—his last two words were spoken mockingly—"is."

"She's a friend of mine. I promised her grandfather I'd find her and bring her back home where she belongs."

"How altogether altruistic! Did you hear him, my dear? Mr. Conrad is a doer of good deeds." Farley placed the tip of an index finger on his chin. "But I wonder. Do you expect, perhaps, some sort of reward for the doing of your good deed, Mr. Conrad? From the grandfather in question? Or, perhaps, from the lady herself? Some friendly sort of recompense from her for your time and trouble, eh?"

Farley's snide words ripped the lid off Gabe's temper, which he had, up until now, kept under firm control. He lashed out, landing a right uppercut on Farley's jaw that snapped the man's head up and sent him staggering backward toward the open door.

Farley reached out and seized the door to steady himself. But his efforts were in vain because Gabe had gone after him and, before he could recover from the shock of the first blow, Gabe had delivered a roundhouse right that slammed the side of Farley's face into the door.

Gabe stepped back as Farley, his hands moving along the smooth surface of the door, slid to his knees and leaned limply against the door for support.

Mrs. Farley brushed past Gabe and went to kneel beside her husband, whose lower lip had been split. "Go," she said over her shoulder to Gabe. "Take your friend and go. Please!"

"Come on," Gabe said to Likes Horses. He took her hand and started for the door.

"No!" Farley cried feebly. He violently pushed his wife aside and reached out to seize Gabe's left leg in both hands.

Gabe halted and stared contemptuously down at Farley a moment before shaking his leg free of the man's frantically grasping hands. "Let's go," he said to Likes Horses and she hurried out the door ahead of him.

Gabe was one step behind her when he heard Mrs. Farley cry, "Look out!"

He spun around to find Farley, still on his knees, holding a double-barreled derringer in his hand. The gun was aimed directly at Gabe, and for a moment he froze. But then, as Farley's finger tightened on the trigger, Gabe threw himself to the floor.

Farley's shot missed Gabe and smashed a stained glass window next to the door.

Gabe came up fast before Farley could fire a second time. He seized the wrist of Farley's gunhand and twisted it savagely.

Farley let out a wail. His eyes squeezed shut. With his left hand he clawed at Gabe's fingers, raking them with his nails and drawing blood.

Gabe twisted Farley's wrist again. This time the gun fell from Farley's hand. Only then did Gabe release his hold on the man's wrist. As he rose, Mrs. Farley bent down to retrieve her husband's gun, straightened and took aim at Gabe.

"Get out of here, Mr. Conrad," she said. "Get out of here right now. Take your friend with you and leave us alone!"

Gabe touched the brim of his hat to her and left the house.

"Shoot him!" Farley screeched to his wife. "Kill him! He invades my home—steals my property—he—"

As Gabe swung into the saddle of his horse, he saw why Farley had suddenly fallen silent. Mrs. Farley had turned and was pointing the derringer at her husband, who still knelt on the floor by the open door, his face florid with rage.

"What do you think you are doing?" Farley barked at his wife. "Are you mad, woman? Stop pointing that gun at me!"

Gabe held out a hand and helped Likes Horses climb up behind him.

"Hurry!" she said to him. "Let us leave here quickly."

But Gabe hesitated, wanting to see how the little drama being enacted in the entrance hall of the house would end. He was somewhat disappointed when Mrs. Farley's finger left the trigger of the derringer. She let the gun clatter to the floor before turning and running down the hall, tears streaming from her eyes.

"True love never runs smooth," Gabe said to himself before wheeling his horse and riding away.

He was not surprised when he heard the sound of a shot come from behind him. "Farley's last stand," he told Likes Horses.

CHAPTER EIGHT

When Gabe decided he had put enough miles between himself and Dade Farley, he drew rein in a wooded glade near a shallow stream and, after helping Likes Horses to step down to the ground, dismounted.

"You alright?" he asked as she stood on the bank of the stream and stared into its clear water. When she didn't answer him, he said, "Whatever happened to you while you were with Farley, it doesn't matter now. It's over and done with. You've got to forget about it and get on with your life."

"I can't forget what happened—what he did to me—what he made me do to him."

Gabe went to where Likes Horses was standing, put his hands on her shoulders and turned her around so that she was facing him. "You *can* forget. You have to. You've got the whole rest of your life to live and you can't let misfortune, no matter what form it takes, pull you down. You do and you won't be good for anything—or anybody."

Likes Horses bit her lower lip and looked away from him.

He took her chin in his hand and turned her head so that she was once again facing him. "What I'm telling you is the truth. You know it is."

"Some things cannot be forgotten," she murmured.

"Then remember them but don't let them destroy your life. They happened. But they won't happen again. You're young. One of these days you're going to meet someone and you're going to fall head over heels in love with him. You'll get married, you and him, and the first thing you know you'll be raising a family. If you let yourself live in the past none of that's going to happen. You'll be living in a dead world among dead things and that's hurtful way to live. Hurtful to you and everybody around you."

"People will know what happened to me."

"They won't. They can't possibly know."

"They will guess and gossip and that will be worse."

"You don't strike me as a weak woman."

Likes Horses' eyes met Gabe's. Suddenly, there was iron in them. "I am not weak."

"Then show me and everybody else how strong you are by refusing to be struck down by one blow, bad as that blow was. Get up. Fight for what's rightfully yours—the future and the hope and happiness it can hold for you if you fight for them."

The iron was still in Likes Horses' eyes when she said, a few thoughtful moments later, "You are right, Long Rider."

Gabe felt the thrill of victory sweep over him. He had worried that whatever bad experience this woman had had at the callous hands of a man like Dade Farley might leave permanent scars on her that would never heal because she would keep picking at them, worrying them, making them bleed again and again, day after unhappy day. But now, looking into her eyes, he knew that was not to be the case and he found the knowledge sweet.

"Yesterday's dead," he told her. "Today's on its way

to being a memory. What counts most—and you should keep this in mind—is tomorrow and all the other tomorrows coming down the pike toward you."

"How did you find me?"

"Well, it wasn't too hard a task, although it wasn't all that easy either." He told her about his search for her, which had finally ended successfully.

"I was afraid that no one would come looking for me. My grandfather is old and the young men the Comancheros took—they could not search for me."

"You mean because Camargo sold them off the same as he did you."

Likes Horses nodded. "I am glad you came looking for me, Long Rider. I am gladder still that you found me and took me away with you."

"So am I. Now I've got a question for you, Likes Horses. What happened to the men of your village—the ones the Apaches sold to Camargo?"

"I do not know. Some men—some white men with guns—came and they took the young men away in wagons, all of them."

"Did you happen to hear any of the white men say anything that might give me some clue as to where they were headed or what they had in mind to do with the men they bought?"

"They made bets among themselves about how long the men they were taking away would last—would live. They said even the strongest men wouldn't last long in the city."

"The city?"

"They said they were going to the city. To a place one of them called Cinnabar City. I do not think there really is such a place. The men laughed when they spoke the name as if it were a joke."

"Cinnabar City," Gabe mused. "I don't recall ever having heard of such a town in these parts. But that doesn't nec-essarily mean there isn't one. Towns spring up out west here like mushrooms after a warm rain. Did you hear any of them say anything else that might help put me onto their trail?"

"One of the men said they were in a hurry to be on their way. He said they had a good fifty miles to travel before nightfall. The man named Camargo asked him why he was in such a hurry and he said he didn't want to still be on the trail at night with a bunch of heathen savages who might try to lift his hair and the hair of the men he had with him."

"Did you see which way they went when they drove off with the men they bought from Camargo?"

"They rode into the setting sun."

"West," Gabe said thoughtfully. "West to a place they called Cinnabar City."

"What are we going to do now?"

"I'm going to take you north to your grandfather and then I'm going to head west and see if I can't find this place called Cinnabar City, and get Sees the Moon and the rest of your young men away from the ones who bought them."

"But, you are one man alone. There were four men who came to Camargo to buy Sees the Moon and the others. There may be other white men at this place they call Cinnabar City. How will you fight them all by yourself?"

"Well, I reckon I'll worry about that bridge when it comes time to cross it."

Likes Horses stepped closer to Gabe and placed her hands on both sides of his face. Drawing his head down toward her, she kissed him on the lips. "I don't want anything to happen to you. I don't want you to be hurt." She kissed him again.

His tongue broke through the barrier of her teeth and it had no sooner done so than she began to suck lustily on it, drawing it all the way into her mouth.

Gabe eased her down to the ground. His hand crept beneath her skirt to caress her thigh and then her hot mound.

He lay down beside her and slid the middle finger of

his right hand into her. She responded instantly and eagerly to his probing. Her warm body squirmed beside him as
her searching lips again found his and locked upon them.
Then, abruptly, she withdrew and Gabe's finger slid out
of her. He wondered if something was wrong but, before
he could ask her if there was, she was slipping out of her
dress and he knew that nothing was wrong. Knew, in fact,
that everything was right as he too slipped out of his clothes
and then flopped back down beside her.

She embraced him and then her hands began to explore
his body. A moment later, her lips joined the explora-
tory expedition. They were everywhere upon him, tasting,
caressing, kissing. Shudders shook him as wave after wave
of pure pleasure washed over him. He was about to cover her
when she scrambled up onto her knees and, straddling him,
touched the tip of his stiff shaft with the tip of her fingers,
causing it to throb. He reached up and took her breasts in
his hands. She moaned with pleasure as he fondled them,
thumbing their brown nipples into erect life. She lowered her
body toward him and he took her left breast in his mouth and
began to suck on it, causing her to moan even louder than
before. Then she withdrew from him and eased up along
his body until the cleft between her legs was directly above
his lips.

As she lowered herself upon him, his tongue shot into her
and began to snake its way about in the hot darkness. She
cried out as he continued his arousing ministrations while
simultaneously caressing both of her breasts. As the scent of
sex swirled around them, Likes Horses drew back until her
knees were once again pressing against the sides of Gabe's
legs. Slowly, she lowered her head. Her lips parted.

He watched as her soft lips closed around the head of his
shaft. He continued watching as she lowered her head still
further until her lips were pressed against the hairy thatch
at the base of his shaft. And then, as her head began to rise
and quickly descend in a swift exciting rhythm, she made
soft mewling sounds, and Gabe, his head thrown back and

his eyes closed, felt himself ascending ecstatic heights until at last he erupted and cried out as Likes Horses' tongue continued to lave the long quivering length of him.

She straightened and looked down at him, a faint smile on her face as she positioned herself above his shaft and then lowered herself onto it, tensing as it gradually disappeared within her.

Gabe had no time to relax after his orgasm because Likes Horses was writhing on him, twisting her pelvis in every possible direction as she emitted a series of grunts.

Then she cried out, a shrill sound, as she achieved the first of what proved to be a pair of orgasms. She cried out even louder as Gabe also climaxed when she did the second time.

Only gradually did her movements begin to slow, and it was several pleasurable minutes before she finally rose and he slid out of her. Then, lying down beside him, her fingers gently caressing his chest, his navel, his now semi-stiff shaft, she sighed and said, "It was good. It was very good."

"For me too," he murmured lazily as he lay there satisfied and spent.

She sighed and lay down on her back, her fingers withdrawing from him.

He gazed lazily off into the distance, watching a cluster of sparrows throw themselves at the sky. He was still idly staring into the distance when he saw a flock of bluejays, closer to where he lay than the sparrows, also fly screeching up into the sky.

He quickly sat up and squinted at the land that lay beneath the flying birds. He saw nothing. But the land was heavily timbered, so that proved nothing. He placed his ear to the ground.

"What is it?" Likes Horses asked him. "What's wrong?"

"Quiet!" He listened. And then leaped to his feet, pulling Likes Horses to her feet as well. "Get dressed. Quickly now!"

She obeyed, her black eyes on him, her brow furrowed with worry that was but one step away from fear.

Gabe was pulling on his boots, hopping from one foot to the other as he did so, when she asked again, "What's wrong?"

"Somebody's coming," he answered, still watching the timbered land where someone had startled the sparrows and jays, sending them all aloft.

Then he saw Dade Farley emerge from the timber. He pointed.

Likes Horses gasped. A hand flew up to cover her mouth. She glanced fearfully at Gabe.

"Farley's not bothering with his derringer this time out," Gabe observed. "He's wearing a two-gun rig and that's a Springfield rifle he's got in his saddle scabbard. "Come on. We've got some hard traveling to do." Gabe leaped into the saddle, gave a hand to Likes Horses and, when she was securely seated behind him, he spurred his bay and they went galloping away from the pursuing and heavily armed Dade Farley.

"Hurry, Long Rider!" Likes Horses cried as they went racing across a stretch of tableland, her arms encircling Gabe's waist. "I don't want him to take me back."

"Don't you fret. He won't take you back. Not unless it's over my dead body."

Gabe, as Likes Horses nervously tightened her hold on him, raked his horse with his spurs, and the animal responded with a renewed burst of speed, its mane flying and its tail held high.

When he spotted the hills that had appeared ahead, he made for them as fast as the bay could go, wanting to get in among them and off the flatland across which he had been traveling because it left him in plain sight of his pursuer, who was now clearly visible far behind him.

The bay tore up the ground as it ran on, with Gabe bent low over the animal's neck and Likes Horses still tightly clutching Gabe's body. Within minutes—minutes that seemed like hours to Gabe—they were in among the sheltering hills and the pine trees growing on their slopes. Gabe drew rein and helped Likes Horses down to the ground.

"Why do we stop here?" she asked him, her nervousness making her voice quaver.

"I'm going to make a stand," Gabe answered, drawing his Winchester from its scabbard. "We can't keep running forever. Take cover over there."

Likes Horses went to a young pine and crouched down behind it as Gabe had directed. Her gaze shifted from him to Farley—who was rapidly approaching the hills—and then back to Gabe again.

He got down on one knee behind a pine and raised his rifle. With his left elbow propped up on his left knee, he squinted through the gun's sight and took aim at Farley. As the man came closer to the hills, he shifted the barrel of his weapon slightly to the right. He fired. His warning shot tore past Farley, causing the man to straighten in his saddle and slow his horse.

Gabe squeezed off a second round. This one, as he intended for it to do, ripped up the ground directly in front of Farley's horse's hooves. The animal balked and reared, almost throwing Farley from the saddle.

But Farley fought the animal and finally won. The horse brought its front hooves crashing down to the ground and then, despite Farley's firm grip on the reins, circled several times, wildly tossing its head as it did so.

Farley lashed his mount with the reins to bring it under control and then went galloping off at a right angle to the trail he had been following. Within seconds he had reached his destination, a hummock covered by a dense growth of manzanita bushes. He got out of the saddle and threw himself flat on the ground, the black barrel of the Springfield rifle he had pulled from his saddle scabbard poking through the evergreens. He fired two shots in quick succession but neither did Gabe any damage.

Gabe returned the fire, breaking off a manzanita branch and sending it flying backward to brush past the half-hidden Farley.

"Send her out here to me, Conrad! If you don't, you're a dead man."

"She's staying with me," Gabe yelled in response to Farley's demand.

Farley fired a third shot. This one tore bark from the tree behind which Gabe had taken cover. Gabe did not immediately return the fire. He maintained his position, waiting to see what Farley would do next. He didn't have to wait long to find out. Farley, crouching low, his body bent nearly double, ran from behind his hummock to another one about thirty yards ahead of him. When he reached it, he dropped down out of sight for a moment and then fired again.

Likes Horses let out a little cry as the round struck Gabe's covering pine again. He straightened and loped over to her. "Take the gun," he told her and thrust it at her. When she had it in her hands, he said, "Keep firing at Farley. Don't kill him. Just keep him pinned down out there. I'll be back."

"But—where are you going?"

"I'll be back," Gabe repeated and went running through the pines. Minutes later, he changed direction, heading at a right angle to his previous path. He raced on and then, when he was far behind Farley's present position, which was off to his left, he changed direction again. This time he headed for the hummock behind which Farley had first taken cover. He ran noiselessly, his eyes on Farley's back, which was visible to him on the left. The man was firing at the spot where he thought Gabe still was. His fire was returned by Likes Horses, who remained safely out of sight.

When Gabe reached Farley's horse, he gave the animal a sharp slap on the rump and sent it trotting away from him. He ran up behind the animal again and repeated the process. This time the startled horse nickered and galloped away, heading back the way Farley had come. Gabe watched it closely, and when it showed signs of slowing he leaned down, tore two clods of earth from the ground and hurled them at the animal, one after the other. Both of them struck their target and had the effect Gabe desired. They sent Farley's horse racing away across the tableland until it disappeared from sight in the distance.

Satisfied that he had accomplished what he had set out to do, Gabe turned and retraced his steps, loping along at a steady pace and carefully keeping out of Farley's sight. He heard the continuing exchange of shots between Farley and Likes Horses, and noted that Farley had not advanced from his position as a result of Likes Horses' sporadic gunfire. By the time he reached her, he was sweating and out of breath.

"I thought you would never return," she told him, smiling at the sight of him. "I did as you asked. Farley has not moved since you left."

"So I see. You did a good job and I appreciate it. Now it's time for us to be moving on again."

"You think we can escape from him? You do not think he will catch up with us, or shoot us from behind?"

"I don't think he'll be a problem to us now. I got rid of his horse." Gabe explained what he had done, and when he finished he took his Winchester from Likes Horses, returned it to his scabbard and then climbed aboard the bay. He helped her climb up behind him and then moved out.

There was silence at first as they left the spot where they had briefly made a stand, and then there came a rash of shots from Farley, which brought a smile to Gabe's face as he thought of the man firing at a target that was no longer where he thought it was. Gabe maintained a steady pace, not wanting to drive his horse too hard now that there was little or no danger of being overtaken by Farley.

He finally drew rein beside a stream, and he and Likes Horses dismounted. He led his bay over to the water and let it drink as he and Likes Horses knelt on either side of the horse and did the same. Then he stripped his saddle and saddle blanket from the animal and, using handfuls of grass, began to wipe the sweaty animal down. Likes Horses took the saddle blanket from him, shook it out and draped it over a low-hanging branch of a locust tree.

Gabe continued wiping down the bay, his thoughts focused on the task that lay ahead of him: finding and rescuing the men who had been taken captive in the Apache attack on the Comanche camp. Once he had returned Likes Horses to her grandfather, he would set out in search of Cinnabar City, where he hoped to find and free the Comanche captives.

The bay's flesh rippled under his hands as he wiped away the last of the animal's sweat and a few stray blades of grass that clung to the animal's hide. He examined its mane and deftly removed a burr he found entangled in it, which had irritated a small spot on the horse's neck. He checked his mount's shoes, lifting first one foot and then the next until he was satisfied that all of them were in sound shape. Straightening, he suddenly became aware that Likes Horses had vanished.

He looked around the area but she was nowhere to be seen. He checked the ground beneath the locust tree and found her footprints. Following the faint trail her moccasins had made in the soft soil, he resisted the impulse to call her name aloud. He didn't want to alert anyone else who might be in the vicinity to his—and her—presence there. Relief flooded him when he met her returning to the spot where they had stopped. In her hands were a number of the short reddish branches of a shrub that had glossy leaves and a number of bright red berries.

"*Salal,*" she said to him, holding up the foliage she had gathered and using the Indian name for what westerners called variously boxberry, creeping snowberry and other names. She handed him a branch and he proceeded to pluck and eat the berries it bore, relishing their spicy flavor and not minding at all their tendency to mealiness.

They walked along together on their way back to the stream and Gabe's horse, both of them hungrily devouring berries as they went. When they reached the stream, they sat down side by side on the bank and continued enjoying their small feast, not saying anything, both of them content to be where they were as the stream whispered wetly past them.

Some time later, when most of the berries had been consumed, Gabe rose and, with Likes Horses anxiously watching him, made his way over to the locust tree where she had hung his saddle blanket. He felt it. It had dried. Likes Horses, finishing the last of the berries, rose and joined him as he folded the blanket and once again placed it on the bay's back. She picked up and handed him his saddle, which he placed on top of the blanket. He bent down and cinched it securely in place. Flipping down his stirrups, he stepped into the saddle and held out a hand to his companion. She climbed up behind him and wrapped her arms around his waist as Gabe lightly touched the bay with his spurs and the horse moved out.

They had not gone far when Likes Horses' arms stiffened around Gabe's waist. "Someone comes," she said uneasily.

"Not someone," Gabe corrected as he drew rein and squinted into the sunlit distance ahead of them. "A bunch of someones." He continued to watch warily, his eyes narrowed, his keen ears picking up the sound of what he estimated must be half a dozen horses, maybe more.

Moments later, the riders came into sight as they rounded a bend and Gabe, when he saw them, muttered an oath.

Likes Horses gave a little cry. "Long Rider, it is—"

"I know who it is," Gabe said and wheeled his horse. Spurring it so hard that he left bloody tracks on the bay's flanks, he rode back the way he had come, as behind him Miguel Camargo shouted an order to the Comancheros he was leading and began to pursue Gabe and Likes Horses.

Even before the first shot sang its deadly song as it went wailing past Gabe, he knew he could not continue his flight. The shot had proved that if proof were needed. The next one might slam into the back of Likes Horses. He glanced

over his shoulder. They were gaining on him. He slowed
his horse and then brought it to a stop.

"Long Rider!" a dismayed Likes Horses cried. "We must
flee!"

"Can't," he said, and told her why they couldn't.

He had barely finished his explanation when the Comancheros were upon them. Camargo, smoking gun in hand,
rode around and around Gabe and Likes Horses, a self-satisfied smile on his face.

"So, Gabe Conrad," he gloated, "we meet again. But not
by accident. We have been looking for you for some time
now."

"Well, you've found me, Camargo."

"Si, that is so, I am most happy to say." The Comanchero
leader halted his horse and sat his saddle in front of Gabe.
"What you did to us, it was a bad thing. When you freed
our Paiute prisoners it could be said and said truthfully that
you stole money from us—the money those prisoners would
have brought when we sold them."

When Gabe said nothing, Camargo continued. "Now that
we have found you again, I see that we have also found
the woman we sold to Dade Farley some time ago. Seeing
her—it makes me see other things as well."

Camargo gestured and the Apache, Cuchillo, rode up to
Gabe and took his rifle out of its scabbard. Sanchez, on the
opposite side, slipped Gabe's revolver from its holster.

"I see," Camargo continued, "that you did not come to
us to be a Comanchero as you claimed. You came to find
out about the woman who now sits behind you with fear
on her pretty face. That is so, si?"

"That's so, yes."

"What is your connection to the Indian woman?"

"I happened to be in her village when the Apaches raided
it. I promised her grandfather I'd find her and bring her back
to him."

"And you did find her."

"That's right, I did."

"But you have not yet returned her to her grandfather." Camargo smiled his mirthless smile again. "And now you never will."

Camargo's words chilled Gabe. "Look," he said to the Comanchero leader, "let her go. Your quarrel's with me. Likes Horses had nothing to do with freeing the Paiutes you bought from those Apaches."

"That is quite true," Camargo agreed almost pleasantly. "But let her go?" He shook his head. "I am afraid I cannot do that. A man does not throw away what is worth good money to him."

Behind Gabe, Likes Horses whimpered.

"Now there is a question that must be answered," Camargo declared. "The question is this: What are we to do with Gabe Conrad, who came to us pretending he wanted to be one of us?"

"Give him to me," Cuchillo demanded.

Camargo glanced at the Indian. "And if I did that you would, my good Cuchillo, cut him into little pieces, si?"

"He would be a long time dying," the Indian muttered balefully, his black eyes boring into Gabe's. "I want revenge for what he did to me back at the ranch."

"We do not have time for inflicting the long death of your tribe, Cuchillo. I am sorry but we must be about our business. We will hang him."

"No." The word seemed to have been torn from Likes Horses' throat. "Take me! Let Long Rider go!"

Before Gabe could stop her, she was down off his horse and throwing herself on her knees before Camargo. Her hands reached up toward the Mexican as she implored him to release Gabe.

"What is this?" Camargo asked, glancing at Gabe. "You call him Long Rider? What does the name mean?"

Speaking swiftly, Likes Horses explained how Gabe had come by the name and, when she had finished doing so, Camargo looked at Gabe and, smirking, said, "So it comes to pass that we are not going to hang a man after all."

"Thank you!" Likes Horses cried, tears spilling from her eyes. "Thank you for sparing Long Rider's life."

"Not so fast, woman," Camargo cautioned. "I did not say we would not hang him. I said we were not about to hang a *man*. Instead, it would seem, we are to hang a hero—and a legend."

Likes Horses dropped her beseeching hands, lowered her head and began to weep openly, the forlorn sound of her crying blending with the harsh sound of Camargo's mocking laughter.

"I will do it," Cuchillo said, picking up the coiled rope that hung from his saddle horn.

"Tie a tight knot," Sanchez called out.

As the other men laughed, Camargo pointed. "Somebody is coming." His hand dropped to the butt of the gun on his hip.

"It's Dade Farley," Sanchez observed. "I'll bet my bottom dollar he's after his woman."

Likes Horses got to her feet and stood beside Gabe's bay as they both watched Farley approach.

When the man rode up to the group, he gave Gabe a withering glance and asked, "What's going on here, Camargo?"

"I have had some difficulties with this man," Camargo answered, indicating Gabe with a sweep of his hand. The Comanchero succinctly explained what he meant.

"He's given me more than my fair share of trouble too," Farley remarked when Camargo fell silent. "As you can see, he ran off with her." He nodded in Likes Horses' direction. "I caught up with them and we shot a few rounds at one another, but my horse went and ran off on me and so did those two." This time he indicated Gabe as well as Likes Horses. "By the time I rounded up my mount, those two were long gone."

"Your horse didn't run off on you, Farley," Gabe said. "I ran him off while Likes Horses used my rifle to keep you pinned down."

"Why you son of a bitch!" Farley exclaimed, going for his gun.

"Leave it leathered, Farley!" Camargo barked.

"I want to kill the bastard," Farley cried. "I want to get even with him for what he's done to me."

"We intend to put him out of action," Camargo said silkily. "We were just about to hang him when you rode up. You're welcome to stay and watch."

There was an expression of disappointment on Farley's face at Camargo's announcement, but he tried his best to hide it as he removed his hand from his gun butt. "Go ahead, hang him high," he said. "I'm going to enjoy watching this."

"It's a pity," Camargo sighed. "Conrad would have made a good Comanchero." He nodded to Cuchillo, who dismounted and strode toward Gabe.

"Once he's dead and done for," Farley said, his tone sharp, his eyes fastened on Gabe's face, "I'll mosey on out of here with her." His eyes shifted to Likes Horses, and in them an ugly fire burned.

"You're wrong on that score, Farley," Camargo said as Likes Horses quickly positioned herself between the still-mounted Gabe and the advancing Cuchillo. "I intend to take her with me."

Farley's eyes widened in surprise. His mouth worked but, at first, no words emerged from it. "What do you mean, you're taking her with you?" he finally managed to ask.

"I mean just what I said. I'm taking her with me."

"But she's mine!"

"Not so, she's mine."

"I bought and paid for her!" Farley protested, his face reddening.

Cuchillo had halted a few feet away from Likes Horses, his eyes shifting back and forth between Camargo and Farley as the two men continued their dispute.

"But you couldn't hold on to her," Camargo reminded Farley. "Now she's mine. I once heard a Philadelphia lawyer say that possession is nine-tenths of the law." Camargo grinned.

"You've got no right to her," Farley argued. "We made a deal."

"So we did, so we did. I'll tell you something, Farley. I'm perfectly willing to make another deal. I'll sell her to you again—for twice the price this time. How does that strike you?"

"That's highway robbery!" Farley spluttered, spraying saliva. "It's not *fair!*"

"That's the deal I'm offering you, Farley," Camargo said flatly. "You can take it or you can leave it. It's all up to you. In the meantime, while you're thinking it over, we've got a hanging to see to, so I don't want to hear one more word out of you about the woman or anything else."

"You won't hear one more word out of me," Farley said, his voice ominously low now.

"That's good. That's not only good, it's sensible."

Farley went for his guns. But he didn't move fast enough. Before his two revolvers had fully cleared leather, Camargo's gun was in his hand and he fired a single shot that struck Farley just above the bridge of his nose.

Farley's hands flew up. His guns sank back down into their holsters. His body flew backward, his legs leaving his stirrups and coming up alongside his horse's neck. He flew backward off his horse. When he hit the ground, his head snapped upward, revealing the round ragged hole in the back of his skull where Camargo's round had exited, and from which bone fragments and bits of gray brain matter had emerged to splatter the ground. His head fell back down and a glassy look entered his eyes. His fingers clawed weakly at the ground for a moment and then were still. His head fell to one side.

"Well, now that we've settled that little dispute," Camargo said, "let's get on with the hanging, gentlemen."

CHAPTER NINE

"No!" Likes Horses cried as Cuchillo made a grab for Gabe.
She fought him, her small fists pummeling his broad chest.
When her efforts had no effect on the Indian, she clawed at
his face with her fingernails. When she drew blood, Cuchillo
cursed. He seized her and flung her to the ground.

Gabe sprang from the saddle and sent his right fist flying
into Cuchillo's face. Cuchillo cursed again, louder and more
volubly this time, and kicked Gabe in the groin.

The blow caused Gabe to double over in pain. As he did
so, clutching his injured genitals, Cuchillo brought a knee
up and slammed it against his lowered chin. The blow sent
agony surging through him as his head snapped back and he
fell to the ground, losing his hat as he did so. He lay there,
doubled up, still clutching his groin, his body convulsing as
a result of the Indian's blows, which had turned his entire
world into one of nothing but searing pain.

Cuchillo kicked him. As Gabe rolled over defensively to
protect his face, Cuchillo bent down and seized his wrists.
He twisted his arms behind his back. Gabe groaned as

Cuchillo rammed a foot into the small of his back and began to tie his hands together behind his back.

"Stop it!" Likes Horses screamed as she got to her feet. Before she could attack Cuchillo a second time, Sanchez grabbed her by the hair and held her nearly immobile, her hands still trying in vain to reach Cuchillo.

Gabe, despite the terrible pain he was suffering, forced himself to concentrate. He held his wrists in such a way that there was a small space between them as Cuchillo bound them together, then cut the rope and proceeded to make a noose at one end of it. When he had fashioned one that suited him, he tossed the other end of the rope over the limb of a tree and then dropped the noose around Gabe's neck. He manhandled Gabe up into the saddle once again, where he sat with his head hanging down. Cuchillo then watched as Camargo stepped forward and reached up to position the noose more precisely. When the rope rose beside and against Gabe's left ear, Camargo stepped back and nodded to Cuchillo.

The Indian was about to tie the free end of the rope to the trunk of the tree when Sanchez suddenly let out a shout. Every Comanchero eye turned to him as Likes Horses continued to bite his hand, forcing him to release her. As Sanchez held his injured hand in his other one and howled wordlessly, Likes Horses ran to where Farley's corpse lay. She dropped down beside it. When she turned around again, she had one of Farley's two revolvers in her hands. She held the gun steady, aiming it first at Sanchez, then at Cuchillo and finally at Camargo.

"Let Long Rider go," she demanded, her eyes as hard as iron. *"Now!"*

"The bitch!" Camargo muttered under his breath. Then, more loudly, he said, "She's gone and got the goddamn drop on us." He walked several paces to his left, away from Gabe and Cuchillo, shaking his head in apparent chagrin.

Likes Horses swiveled her body, the barrel of Farley's gun in her hand following Camargo.

Cuchillo chose that moment to act. He lashed out with the free end of his hanging rope. It knocked the gun from Likes Horses' hand. He was about to strike her again when Likes Horses leaped to her feet and went racing into the woods and disappeared.

Sanchez and one of the other men started to go after her. But Camargo halted them by holding up his hand. "Let her go. She won't get away from us. We'll catch up with her. But first—hang him high, Cuchillo."

The Indian, beginning to grin, tied the end of the rope to the trunk of the tree. As Gabe raised his head to get one last glimpse of the glorious blue sky above him, Cuchillo slapped the bay's rump. The horse let out an explosive snort and then broke into a gallop.

Gabe was pulled from the saddle. His body swung back and forth at the end of the rope. As his air supply was cut off, a fire hotter than any he had ever known began to burn in his lungs.

"Adios, Conrad," Camargo said, giving Gabe a mocking salute. Then he mounted his horse and rode out, followed immediately by his Comancheros, as they all set out in pursuit of Likes Horses.

The sound of their galloping horses was drowned out for Gabe by the louder pounding of the blood in his brain as his body spun first one way, then the other at the end of the rope. He fought to retain consciousness as the world began to blur around him. It went in and out of focus as he twisted his hands, turned them, fought to free them from the rope that bound them.

Using the little space he had managed to keep between his wrists when Cuchillo had bound them, Gabe pulled his hands as far apart as they would go and tried desperately to stretch the rope just far enough to be able to slide one of his hands through.

He felt the rope give a little. He increased his efforts as he tried simultaneously to draw precious air into his straining lungs. He jerked his right arm upward as hard as he could.

His hand slid halfway through the rope. He jerked his arm again, straining as hard as he could, his eyes squeezed shut. A moment before he succeeded in freeing his hand, he felt his tongue jut out through his parted lips, as often happened to hanged men. He raised both of his hands, the rope still looped loosely around his left wrist, and gripped the rope just above his head. He held on to it as tightly as he could, his strength draining away and leaving him weak.

If he could just remain conscious for another few minutes—if he could muster just enough strength to accomplish the forbidding task he had set for himself—

He pulled on the rope with both hands, raising his body. His action loosened, if only slightly, the noose around his neck. He placed one hand above the other as he continued to haul himself up toward the tree limb over which the rope had been thrown. When he had almost reached the limb, he paused. Holding onto the rope with his right hand, he clawed frantically at the noose around his neck. As he loosened it, he sucked precious air into his lungs, making gasping sounds as he did so. His heart slammed against his ribs, seemingly ready to burst at any moment.

Still gasping but able to breathe now, if painfully, he continued his hand-over-hand ascent until he reached the tree limb above his head. He gripped it with both hands and deliberately began to swing his entire body back and forth. When he had gathered sufficient momentum, he swung himself up onto the limb, grasping it with both hands and wrapping both legs around it. He lay there, his body stretched out along the length of the limb, slipped the noose from around his neck, and shut his eyes. He concentrated on breathing. In. Out. Never mind the fire that still burned in his lungs. Never mind the sharp pain in his neck, the result of severe rope burns. He was alive. His heart had not burst. His lungs had not given out on him.

He lay there on the limb, gripping it tightly to keep from falling, for what seemed to him to be an eternity. But he did not trust himself to move. Not at first. Only gradually, as his breathing began to slow and his heart stopped pounding and began to beat normally once again, did he open his eyes. Then he gingerly began to ease along the limb toward the tree's trunk. When he reached it, he was about to climb down to the ground when he was suddenly overcome with nausea. He retched, his entire body heaving, the contents of his stomach splattering on the ground below. When his body had stopped heaving and he could breathe normally again, he cautiously climbed down from the tree. The instant his boots touched solid ground, an overwhelming weakness washed over him. His knees buckled and he slumped down on the ground. He sat there, leaning one shoulder against the trunk of the tree until the weakness passed.

He looked around him and saw that the Comancheros had stripped Farley's corpse of the man's two-gun rig and had taken his rifle. Gabe realized then they had taken his horse too. His hat lay where it had fallen earlier. He got unsteadily to his feet, went to it and clapped it back on his head.

Likes Horses, he thought. Had the Comancheros caught her? Or had she escaped from them? He had to find her. He put one foot in front of the other. He took another step. Then, another. When he was sure he was not going to lose consciousness and was sure too that his legs and tortured lungs were not going to give out on him, he began to follow the plain trail left by the Comancheros.

His lungs seemed to blaze as he began to run. He was forced to slow down to ease the burning sensation he was experiencing. He walked on at a brisk pace, trying to ignore the pain flaring in his neck caused by the collar of his shirt chafing against the flesh there that had been badly burned by the hanging rope. Impatient with his slow progress, he began to run again. The pain in his lungs returned and he slowed, settling for a lope instead of a run.

The sign he was following was clear. The Comancheros had made no effort to hide their trail. They no doubt figured, he thought as he loped on, that they needn't worry about anybody being on their backtrail. Not with Farley shot and Gabe hanged, they needn't. Well, they were wrong. They should have stayed around after they strung him up to make sure he'd died.

Less than an hour later, he came upon a camp the Comancheros had established at the edge of a stand of manzanita bushes. There was a spring there bubbling up out of the ground in a kind of rocky grotto. They had built a fire and put their horses, including Farley's and Gabe's, out to graze the grass that grew lushly just beyond the spring.

Likes Horses was with them, sitting by herself, her arms wrapped around her knees, her head bent. Gabe took cover behind the manzanita bushes and prepared to wait for dark. When it came, he would make his move.

The time passed slowly while he waited. The sun seemed to him to be stuck in the sky. He was convinced it hadn't moved for over an hour. But at last it set and purple shadows spread out across the land. The Comancheros were roasting corn and baking potatoes as they talked among themselves. Occasionally they gestured toward Likes Horses, and one of them said something that brought laughter to the lips of his companions.

When the purple shadows had turned black and the moon and stars had appeared in the sky, Gabe left his shelter behind the bushes and circled around them, heading for Likes Horses in the distance. He gave the camp a wide berth as he practically crawled along the ground in order not to be seen by the men gathered around the cookfire.

He halted when he was within twenty feet of Likes Horses, then slowly began moving toward her, careful not to make any noise, hating even the soft swishing sound the long grass made as he moved cautiously through it. By the time he reached her, the moon had vanished behind clouds that were scudding across the sky.

He put out a hand and clapped it over her mouth. At the same time, he whispered, "Don't make a sound. It's me, Long Rider."

Likes Horses' eyes had opened and were filled with fright until she heard his voice, then were able to see his face in the darkness as he brought it down close to her own.

He removed his hand from her mouth and, still keeping his head next to hers, said, "We're getting out of here. We'll go get my horse and Farley's and be on our way."

"They will catch us."

"They haven't even posted a guard. Don't worry. Keep low and let's go." He took her by the hand and she rose and followed him, both of them crouching as they hurried around the perimeter of the camp on their way to where the horses, huge black shapes in the night, were quietly grazing.

Likes Horses suddenly lost her balance and fell, almost taking Gabe down with her because of his hold on her hand. Both of them remained motionless as they watched the men around the camp to see if any of them gave any indication of having heard the thud Likes Horses' body had made when it hit the ground. None of the men moved or even looked away from the fire.

Gabe helped Likes Horses to her feet. Together they headed for the horses and had almost reached them when Sanchez stepped out from behind the thick trunk of a shin oak. He threw away the corn shuck he had used to wipe himself and pulled up his trousers. He almost dropped them again when he saw Gabe and Likes Horses standing motionless not ten feet away from him.

"Hey, the camp!" he yelled at the top of his voice. *"Hey, the camp!"*

"Run!" Gabe said to Likes Horses. "Over that way!"

They ran and the men who had been seated around the camp fire ran after them, as did Sanchez once he had gotten his trousers buttoned. Within minutes, Gabe and Likes Horses were run to ground by Sanchez and the men he had alerted. Moments later, they were surrounded by the Comancheros, all of whom had their guns in their hands.

"What the hell is he, a goddamned ghost?"

The remark had come from Cuchillo who, like the others, was staring in disbelief at Gabe and all but ignoring Likes Horses, who stood by his side.

"He looks alive enough to me," Camargo muttered. "Maybe a little worse for the wear but alive and obviously kicking. How did you survive Cuchillo's rope, Conrad?"

Gabe remained silent as he put a protective arm around Likes Horses.

"Never mind," Camargo said dismissively. "It doesn't matter. What does matter is that you are here among us again and we must once again dispose of you—for certain this time."

"We going to hang him again?" an eager Cuchillo wanted to know.

"None of us has a rope," Sanchez said.

"No matter," Camargo responded. "We won't need one."

"You're going to shoot him this time?" Sanchez prompted.

Camargo shook his head. "The bullet would probably pass through and leave unharmed a man who can't be hanged. Our friend, Conrad, seems to lead a charmed life. Well, we will see how long that life of his will last when he becomes a citizen of Cinnabar City."

"Where's this Cinnabar City?" Gabe asked.

"You'll find out soon enough," Camargo answered. "We'll be there in the morning." He turned to Cuchillo. "Guard Conrad carefully so that he does not escape during the night, with or without the woman he seems bound and determined to rescue from our nefarious clutches." He laughed happily at his own deliberately melodramatic words. "If you let him bamboozle you a second time, Cuchillo, I will have to wonder if you are indeed fit to be a Comanchero."

"He won't pull any tricks on me tonight," the Indian assured Camargo, his icy eyes on Gabe. "If he does, I will kill him."

"Sanchez."

"Si?"

"Guard the woman. I don't want to have to chase after her again. Do you understand?"

"Si, I understand." Sanchez went to where Likes Horses was standing with Gabe's arm around her and seized her by the hair. He marched her over to the fire, where he threw her to the ground and stood over her with his gun still drawn.

Cuchillo stayed behind as Camargo and the others made their way back to the fire, holstering their guns as they went. "Do not try to get away from me tonight," he muttered to Gabe. "It would give me great pleasure to kill you. Move!"

Gabe, responding to the Indian's snarled order, walked, with Cuchillo right behind him, to the opposite side of the fire from where Likes Horses was being guarded by Sanchez.

"Five dollars says he won't last thirty days in Cinnabar City," Vickers said to his fellow Comancheros, who were once again seated around their fire.

"He's a strong buck," Sanchez commented, squinting at Gabe across the fire's flames. "I'll take your bet, Vickers, and double it."

"You've just thrown away ten dollars," Vickers told Sanchez. "He may be a barn-shouldered bastard and have legs like the trunks of two young trees, but Cinnabar City's been the death of men even better built than he is, and ones, I'm willing to wager, with twice as much stamina. Some of them didn't last a week."

"We'll see, won't we?" remarked Sanchez.

Gabe, hunkered down only a foot away from Cuchillo, who loomed over him as he stood guard on his prisoner, wondered what fate awaited him. He was certain it would not be a pleasant one, not when the Comancheros were betting on not whether he would survive the place they called

Cinnabar City, but how long it would take him to die there. A chill coursed through him that the nearness of the fire could do nothing to dispel. He glanced over to where Likes Horses was sitting so forlornly on the ground watching him. In his mind, he severely castigated himself for his failure to rescue her—not once, but twice. He gave Likes Horses a smile that he meant to be reassuring. She didn't return it.

They were on the trail before first light the next morning. Before long, they were making their way through the foothills of a low mountain range. The going was difficult and twice they were stopped by armed sentries posted on peaks, who let them pass only after Camargo had identified himself and his men.

Gabe, forced to ride in the midst of the Comancheros with Likes Horses so that they had no chance to escape from their captors, was surprised to see, from a ridge they had just topped, a number of glowing furnaces dotting the valley below.

"Welcome to Cinnabar City," Camargo said to him as they rode down from the ridge and into the valley.

Gabe coughed as the wind suddenly shifted and he inhaled throat-searing smells that was rising from the furnaces. When Camargo called a halt, he studied the men, all of them Comanches from Chief Ten Bears' Antelope Band. They were moving about near the furnaces, which, he could now see, were retort smelters. The men, all of whom had haggard faces and emaciated bodies clothed in rags, fed wood to the furnaces, while other men, many of them trembling uncontrollably, set out rows of iron flasks on wooden tables placed near the smelters. Overseeing them were a number of heavily armed guards.

A man emerged from a large log building and, when he saw the Comancheros, waved and headed for them.

"Morning, Camargo," he said when he reached them. "I wasn't expecting a visit from you this morning."

"We have a new man for you, Rossiter," Camargo said, indicating Gabe with a nod of his head. "His name's Conrad. I'll take fifty dollars for him."

"You're upping the price from forty, are you?"

"For this one, yes. He is something special. Look at him. He's strong as an ox—stronger."

Rossiter dug into his pocket and came up with the money, which he handed to Camargo.

"He'll give you a run for your money, Rossiter," Camargo promised. "Now it's time we were heading home." He turned his horse and rode back the way he had come with Likes Horses and his Comancheros.

"Get down," Rossiter ordered, and when Gabe had dismounted, Rossiter summoned a guard to lead Gabe's bay away to join the many other horses corraled behind the log building.

Gabe said, "Camargo told me this place is called Cinnabar City. How come?"

"Because we mine cinnabar here," Rossiter replied. "We dig it out of that big open pit over there."

Gabe looked in the direction Rossiter had pointed and saw the deep bowl-like depression in the ground.

"We sell the quicksilver we get when the cinnabar's been smelted down and stored in those iron flasks you see over there," Rossiter added. "It's a money-making operation, I assure you, since we don't have to pay fellas like you to dig the ore out of the pit yonder or pay the men who smelt it. Neither do we pay the men we set to gathering wood for the smelters or the ones we got weaving the baskets used to carry the ore from the pit to the smelters."

"Slave labor," Gabe muttered.

"You got it, Conrad."

"Those men at the smelters over there," Gabe said. "They look to me to be in pretty bad shape."

"Oh, they are," Rossiter agreed. They've got mercury poisoning from roasting the ore. Most of them have tried to escape, or else they've given the guards headaches of one kind or another. So we tame 'em by putting them to work smelting the cinnabar, and that tames 'em fast, I can tell you. They also die just about as fast from mercury poisoning. But that's no big problem for us. We can always buy new laborers from Camargo. Big strong fellas like yourself usually last a while. Maybe you will too, Conrad, before you finally drop.

"Stand down," Rossiter ordered Gabe. "You can get yourself a pick over there at that shed. Once you've got it, get your ass down there into that pit."

Gabe hesitated a moment and then started for the shed.

"Conrad."

Gabe turned back to face Rossiter.

"If you make trouble—or if you try to escape—you'll die with so much lead in your body that your soul will sink straight down to hell. That's a promise."

Gabe turned and headed for the shed. He was handed a pick by an armed man and then made his way to the pit.

He halted at its rim and stared down at the men who were making their way down the pit's sloping sides, some of them stumbling and rolling down to the bottom. Then he suddenly found himself toppling down into the pit, because one of the guards ringing its perimeter had slammed a boot against his buttocks and shoved.

He collided with one of the workers in the pit when he hit bottom and knocked the man to the ground. He got to his feet and helped the Indian up, as the guard who had kicked him shouted at him, "That'll learn you not to shilly-shally when there's a day's work to be done!"

Gabe glared up at the guard in silence, retrieved the pick he had dropped and began to dig into the side of the pit. He dislodged chunks of earth that were speckled with bright red crystals and occasional red or brown masses of earth. He continued to dig as an Indian he did not recognize appeared at his side and began to shovel cinnabar into a crudely woven basket which, when he had filled it to the rim, he carried up the slope and over to the smelters.

Gabe had been digging for hours, sweat pouring down his face and soaking his shirt, when he heard his name called. Not Gabe Conrad, but Long Rider. He straightened and saw Sees the Moon coming down into the pit toward him.

"Long Rider, what are you doing here? How did you come here? What has happened to you?"

"Whoa," Gabe said. "One thing at a time." He told Sees the Moon all that had happened to him, and when he had finished, the Comanche shook his head and said, "It is a sad thing that you too have come here as have those of us the Apaches captured."

"What—"

"Keep working," Sees the Moon warned Gabe, "or one of those guards up there on the rim of the pit will give you trouble."

"What are our chances of getting out of this hellhole?" Gabe asked, swinging his pick again.

"We cannot escape, Long Rider." Sees the Moon began to fill the basket he had with him with ore. "We will die here, you and I. All of the men here do. Some sooner. Some later."

"Well, my friend, I, for one, do not intend to die here. I think what you and I ought to do is round up your friends, and then we can try to escape from this place."

Sees the Moon, bent over his ore basket, shook his head. "The guards who work for Rossiter are everywhere, even in the mountains. Any one of them would shoot us down like dogs if we tried to run away. And we have no weapons."

"We have picks. Shovels."

"What good are a few picks and shovels against guns, Long Rider? No, we are trapped here and there is only one way for us to get out of Cinnabar City, and that is by dying." Sees the Moon hoisted the basket onto his shoulder and began to climb slowly up the sloping side of the pit.

"Wait!" Gabe called out to him. He hurried up the slope after the Comanche, who had halted and was waiting for him. "I made a promise to Chief Ten Bears," he said when he reached him. "I promised him I'd do my damnedest to get you and the rest of the men the Apaches took—Likes Horses too—back for him. I still mean to keep that promise. I need your help, Sees the Moon. I need your help and the help of every other Comanche warrior to get out of here and back to your village. Will you help me?"

Sees the Moon hesitated. Then, as he opened his mouth to speak, he was silenced by the sound of men shouting and then the sound of a round being fired by one of the guards.

Both men turned and saw a scarecrow of a man whose bony arms were flapping and whose ragged clothes were fluttering as he fled from the rim of the cinnabar pit toward the distant mountain range.

"He's making a run for it," Gabe commented, excitement in his voice. "I hope he makes it."

But the would-be escapee didn't make it. A round from a guard's carbine struck him, lifted him off the ground and then threw him facedown upon it.

Gabe cursed under his breath.

"The wheel!" shouted the guard who had shot the Comanche. He barked an order and the two slave laborers he had designated detached themselves from the crowd and picked up the limp body of the man on the ground and carried it away. Other guards herded the other workers, Gabe and Sees the Moon among them, in the direction the two men carrying the wounded man had gone.

"What's going on?" Gabe asked Sees the Moon.

"I do not know. But I have heard the guards speak of the wheel. They said—That must be it."

Gabe gazed in the direction Sees the Moon was pointing and saw a wagon wheel mounted on its axle, which had been driven into the ground so that the wheel was parallel to the ground and some two feet above it. Spaced beneath a portion of the wheel's circumference, two iron stakes sprouted a good five inches from the ground.

"What the hell kind of contraption is that?" Gabe asked as he halted near the wheel, but Sees the Moon, instead of answering him, merely shook his head.

"Put him on it!" ordered the guard who had shot the would-be escapee.

Obeying the guard's order, the two men carrying the hapless slave laborer forced him down upon the wheel. Once his back was upon it, they proceeded to tie his hands above his head to two of the wheel's wooden spokes with lengths of rope given them by one of the guards.

The wounded Comanche on the wheel struggled feebly. He cried out first for help, then for mercy. He received neither. Blood flowed freely from a bullet wound in his shoulder and soaked his ragged shirt. He kicked at his captors as each of them seized one of his legs, but they nevertheless managed to tie his ankles to the two stakes that were driven into the ground. When their task was finished, they stepped back and melted into the crowd of prisoners surrounding the wheel.

Two burly guards stepped up to the wheel, got a grip on it and then began to turn it slowly in a counterclockwise direction.

The body of the man tied to the wheel began to twist to one side because his feet were tied to the stakes in the ground.

He began to cry out then, his piercing screams the only sound to be heard except for the faint creaking of the wheel as it continued to turn on its obviously unoiled axle.

"Lord a'mighty!" Gabe muttered under his breath, his face pale. "They're fixing to tear him apart!"

The man on the wheel twisted his head from side to side, his body grotesquely contorted. His lips worked wordlessly and then a long-drawn-out groan issued from between them. His groan became a shrill scream when the two sweating guards gave the wheel another half-turn.

Gabe took a firm step forward and then another, his hands fisted at his sides.

Sees the Moon seized him by the shoulders to stop him in his tracks. "They will shoot you if you try to stop this," the Comanche warned in an urgent whisper.

Gabe knew his friend was right but still he wanted to—

He stood stiffly and stared in horror as the left thigh bone of the victim tore through the man's flesh. He couldn't take his eyes from the awful sight of the blood running down the broken white bone as it jutted upward at an ugly angle from the bound man's leg.

"That ought to do it!" shouted the guard as the Comanche being tortured gave a series of shrill screams.

The two men who had been turning the wheel stepped away from it.

The guard who had just given the order to halt the terrible proceedings scanned the faces of the prisoners. Then, shouting above the sound of the screaming man on the wheel, he said, "Now, should any of you take a notion to try what he just did—" he pointed to the broken body bleeding on the wheel, "that there's what you'll get when we catch you. And catch you we damn well will! Nobody's ever escaped from Cinnabar City. Now, back to work, the lot of you. *Move!*"

"Come, Long Rider," Sees the Moon said.

But Gabe stood his ground, his eyes fastened on the man on the wheel, who seemed to have fainted.

He didn't move a muscle as the other slave laborers began to return to their work. He strained to make out the words the prisoner, who had become conscious again, was murmuring as his head lolled from side to side and he bared his teeth in a lip-twisting grimace. Gabe took a step closer to the bound man, ignoring Sees the Moon, who was urging him to return to the cinnabar pit.

"Help me."

The breathy and barely audible plea reached Gabe's ears, but he could think of no way to help the Indian on the wheel. At that moment, the broken-bodied man's head flopped to one side and his half-closed eyes came to rest on Gabe, who now stood alone where a moment ago there had been a crowd.

"Shoot me," the man pleaded pitifully.

Gabe's right hand dropped to his hip—and touched the worn spot on his jeans where his holster had once rested.

"Please. The pain—" A scream ripped from the victim's lips.

Gabe could barely endure the agonized look the tormented man gave him. He could only stare at the man's thigh bone jutting skyward through sundered flesh—a ghastly symbol of the awful agony the man had endured, and was still enduring.

"Have mercy on me," the man pleaded.

More words came then, harsh and brutal words, from the guard who was fast approaching the spot where Gabe stood. *"Get back to work!"*

Gabe saw the guard and the Remington .45 in the man's dirty hand. His eyes flicked back to meet the imploring eyes of the man on the wheel, the eyes that were crazed with unendurable pain. He waited another split second until the guard was almost upon him and then he lunged at the man, ripping the gun from his hand. He turned, took swift and accurate aim and fired.

The body of the man on the wheel lurched. An abortive cry escaped his lips. Then he went limp, his agony at last ended by the bullet Gabe had put in his brain.

Gabe spun around, the guard's gun still in his hand. Before he could use it the guard he had taken it from seized his wrist and twisted it. The gun roared. The round went harmlessly into the ground just as another guard appeared. Gabe saw the newly arrived guard's rifle stock come slamming down toward him. Before he could get out of its way, he felt it strike his skull. He grunted as pain roared through his head, and darkness came rushing down upon him in the pain's red wake, sending him spinning away into a world where there were no guards and no wheels on which living men could be shattered.

CHAPTER TEN

Gabe regained consciousness slowly. As he did so he became aware of the pain that flared in his skull as a result of the blow from the guard's rifle stock that he had taken—how long ago?

He sat up, feeling as if his head was about to burst, and cradled his head in his hands.

"Get up!"

The words had been snarled by the guard who had struck him. "Now that you've finished your nap, it's time to get back to work."

Gabe slowly got to his feet and looked around. He saw the familiar sights of the cinnabar pit—the smelters, the slave laborers wearily going about their assigned tasks, the log house that sheltered the mine's guards.

"Get down in the pit," the guard ordered, jabbing Gabe in the ribs with the barrel of his rifle.

But before Gabe could take more than a dozen steps in the direction of the pit, Rossiter appeared and bellowed, "You!"

Gabe turned to face him.

"The pit's too easy a job for a troublemaker like you, Conrad. You'll work the smelters from now on. Next time you decide to make a ruckus, you'll be dead before it starts. You got that?"

Gabe didn't bother to answer. He went over to the smelters, where he was shown by one of the Comanches he knew by sight what he was supposed to do. He spent the rest of the day shoveling cinnabar ore mixed with lime into the firebox of the smelter he had been assigned to, and periodically feeding its fire with cordwood he took from a nearby stack. He worked steadily and in silence under the hot sun, trying in vain to ignore the pain in his head. His mind became numb as he continued performing his repetitive tasks, until he was aware of nothing but the occasional cackling cough of one of the nearby workers, the crackling of the flames in the smelters' fireboxes, the debilitating heat thrown off by those fires, and the stench of the fumes from the cinnabar ore that seared his throat and nose and made his eyes water badly.

That night, after wolfing down a bowl of thin gruel and devouring a hard piece of bread from which he first had to pick out the weevils infesting it—the only rations he and the other men were given—he stretched out on the ground and closed his eyes. But sleep would not come to him despite his exhaustion. The pain that still throbbed in his head drove sleep away.

"Long Rider? Are you awake?"

"I am." Gabe turned his head and stared at Sees the Moon, who was kneeling on the ground beside him, the bright red glow of the flames in the smelters' fireboxes illuminating his features.

"I came here to tell you that I have spoken to the other men. We will fight the guards so that we all may escape from here."

"I thought you seemed opposed to the idea when I mentioned it to you. How come the change of heart?"

"You shamed us all."

"I did? How?"

"We saw what you did to help that man who was on the wheel. None of us dared do anything to help him. You risked your own life to deliver him from a life that was far worse than the death you gave him. I went to talk to the other men. We decided we must escape. So we will fight with you against the guards."

"You fellows all know, I reckon, that you'll be risking your lives if you do. Those guards've got more guns than a hound has fleas."

"I don't want to die—"

"Nobody does."

"—but I don't want to live like this either. All the other men, they feel the same way. We know that even if we do not fight, we will soon die if we stay here. The guards will work us to death. So even though none of us has the courage that you have, Long Rider—"

"No man knows how much courage he has or hasn't got until it's tested."

"You will lead us then?"

"Go round up the rest of the men you talked to and bring them here. We'll have us a war council."

Sees the Moon started to say something but instead reached out and mutely squeezed Gabe's shoulder. Then he was gone, a shadow moving swiftly among other shadows through the firelit night.

Gabe didn't have long to wait. The men came to him one by one, stealthily, silently. When they had all assembled, including Sees the Moon, Gabe said, "Now then, let's get right to it. Do any of you have any ideas about how we ought to go about getting ourselves out of here?"

His question set up a discussion that lasted for the better part of an hour. Numerous proposals were put forward and either accepted or rejected by a consensus of the group after the pros and cons of each had been judiciously weighed and debated.

"Then this is what we've got," Gabe stated when they had all finally agreed upon the outlines of their escape attempt. "We'll make our move at first light, which is when you say the guard changes, when the day men take over from the night men. It ought to be a good time because both sets of guards'll be sleepy, both those coming off duty and those just about to go on duty."

He continued outlining the plan they had made and assigning duties to each of the Indians involved. When he had finished there was nothing to do but wait for first light, and wait they did.

Through what remained of the night some of the men talked in low tones about anything but the impending battle, but most of them sat in silence or tried to sleep, each man alone with his thoughts.

They glanced time and time again toward the east, and they turned as one toward Gabe when the first gray streaks of light began to brighten the eastern horizon.

Gabe neither moved nor spoke until several more minutes had passed and the first of the guards began to emerge from the log building to begin the new day's shift. Then, led by Gabe, the Comanches rose and made their way to their prearranged positions.

"You ready?" Gabe asked Sees the Moon. When the Comanche nodded, he said, "Let's go then."

They started for the log building, wending their way among the laborers who were being prodded awake by guards' rifle butts and boots.

Gabe, as he walked, glanced over his shoulder and was pleased to see that two of the Comanches had reached the smelter that stood closest to the cinnabar pit. Looking to the left, he saw other Comanches in position near each of the day shift's guards that they had chosen as their targets. He walked a few more steps and then, putting two fingers between his teeth, he gave the prearranged signal to start the action that would lead to their escape attempt—a shrill whistle.

In response, Comanches attacked their chosen targets—the individual guards—using pieces of cordwood they had concealed on their persons. Two of the Comanches overturned the smelter near the cinnabar pit, sending a shower of sparks and clouds of smoke up into the air.

The guards were shouting excitedly as they tried to defend themselves from the attacking Comanches. Two went down, knocked senseless by Comanches wielding cordwood like war clubs. A shot was fired by one of the guards before his rifle was wrested from his hands by a war-whooping Comanche, who used it to knock the man off the rim of the cinnabar pit and down into it. Then it was the Comanche who fired the rifle and dropped a guard who was taking aim at Sees the Moon.

Gabe and Sees the Moon reached the log building and took up positions on either side of its door. As the night guards, who had just finished their shift, came running out of the door to see what had caused the commotion outside, both men systematically tripped and then disarmed them. Then Sees the Moon and Gabe ran with the weapons they had confiscated and distributed them to the Comanches for use in the continuing assault.

Smoke from the smelter was filling the area, making it hard to see. Shots were being fired and Gabe saw a Comanche go down and not get up again.

"Look out, Long Rider!" one of the Comanches yelled.

Gabe spun around and saw a disarmed guard running toward him. Although the guard's gun was gone, he had taken the hatchet from the chopping block next to the pile of cordwood and was coming at Gabe with the weapon raised high above his head.

Gabe used the revolver he had confiscated from one of the guards to drop the man in his tracks. As the man went down and the hatchet fell from his hand, Sees the Moon picked it up and hurled it at a guard who had suddenly appeared on the roof of the log building, a rifle in his hands. The blade of the hatchet buried itself in the man's forehead, almost splitting his skull in two. He fell forward and then rolled down off the roof to the ground.

Gabe looked around him and was pleased by what he saw. Through the smoke he could make out the ring of armed Comanches standing on the rim of the cinnabar pit, their guns trained on the guards—and on Rossiter—whom they had herded down into it. With Sees the Moon by his side, he loped over to the pit and looked down.

"Rossiter," he said, "your little slave labor game is over. It is, at least, as far as me and these men with me are concerned. We're riding out of here now. But let me give you and your boys a word of warning. If any of you come out of that pit before the sun rises, we'll shoot your eyes out. Do I make myself clear, Rossiter?"

The man grunted something unintelligible.

"Can't understand you, Rossiter."

"You've made yourself clear as crick water, Conrad," an angry Rossiter shouted.

Gabe beckoned and then, as he ran toward the corral behind the log building, the Comanches followed him. He was gratified to find, when he reached the corral, that the two Comanches assigned to it when the assault began had, as they had been directed to do, saddled his bay and fashioned rope bridles for the horses the Comanches would use in their escape.

"Let's be on our way!" he shouted as he ran into the corral and leaped aboard his bay. Raising his rifle high above his head, he gestured with it and the Comanches boarded the mounts that had been made ready for them by their two companions and rode barebacked out of the corral behind him, most of them whooping loudly in sheer joy at the success of their escape attempt.

Gabe led them north into the foothills. "We don't want to alert the sentries in these mountains to the fact that we're free," he told the men riding with him. "Keep your eyes peeled. If you spot a sentry and he tries to take you down, shoot him."

Ten minutes later, as they ascended the mountains, one of the Comanches did just that. A sentry perched in a treetop took aim and fired at the group. He hit one of the Comanches in the shoulder. One of the man's companions promptly returned the fire. A whoop of unadulterated delight went up from the Comanches when the sniper fell from his perch and hit the ground with an unnerving booming sound.

Gabe again asked for silence and again the Comanches obeyed, suppressing their excitement and giving it no voice. They rode on warily but encountered no more sentries. Gabe speculated that they might have passed such men without having seen them and that the men, seeing the many Indians led by a lone white man, might have decided not to show themselves and risk getting killed by the superior force passing by them. In any case, the ride up and then down the mountains proved uneventful following the exchange of shots with the single sentry they had encountered.

When the mountains had been left behind them, Gabe drew rein and brought his bay to a halt.

Sees the Moon, surprised by his move, also halted and so did the other Comanches.

"What is wrong?" Sees the Moon asked, frowning and glancing back over his shoulder to see if they were being pursued.

"Nothing's wrong," Gabe replied. "It's just that we've reached the place where I've got to leave you."

"Why?"

"I'm going to get Likes Horses away from the Comancheros. I promised Chief Ten Bears I'd bring her back to him and I hope to make good on my promise if I possibly can."

Sees the Moon exchanged glances with the other men and then said to Gabe, "We will go with you."

Gabe started to protest, to say that he knew the Comanches wanted to get home, but Sees the Moon silenced him by saying, "You have helped us, Long Rider. Now it is our

turn to help you. It is not good for you to go alone to the
Comancheros. They outnumber you. With us to help you,
you maybe will not die when you try to take Likes Horses
away from them."

Well, Gabe thought, that's putting the truth right up front
where it belongs. *With us to help you, you maybe will not
die when you try to take Likes Horses away from them.*

"Come on then."

As Gabe rode out, the Comanches followed him, the
sound of their horses' pounding hooves striking the ground
an ominous thunder in the air as they headed for the lair of
the Comancheros.

When they neared the mouth of the canyon that led to the
valley where the Comancheros were headquartered, Gabe
called a halt. "We're going to have to circle around instead
of going in through that canyon. They've always got a guard
posted up on top of that mesa. He fires a shot to warn those
in the ranch that somebody's coming, and I don't want our
arrival announced. What I want to do is surprise Camargo
and his boys. Get the drop on them if we can before any serious shooting starts. So we'll come down on the ranch from
that hill that rises behind it. The guard up on the mesa'll
have a lot harder time seeing us if we go that way because
there's good cover on the hill, trees and such. Still we'll
have to take care not to be seen."

They wheeled their mounts and rode away from the canyon's mouth. It took them over an hour to circle around and
reach the hill that loomed behind the Comancheros' ranch
house.

"We'll leave our horses just below the rise up there,"
Gabe said as they began to climb the hill. "I'll make my
way down the other side of the rise and get into the ranch
house. If there's trouble—and there very well might be—
I'm counting on you to back me up."

"I will go down with you," Sees the Moon declared. "I
will stand guard while you go inside."

"Good idea. Okay, here we are. Dismount, men."

They did, after which Gabe deployed the Comanches just below the ridge line. "Keep careful watch," he told them. "Like as not, me and Sees the Moon won't be needing your help, but it's good to know you'll be here if it turns out we do need you." Then he and Sees the Moon crept up to the ridge line and peered down at the ranch house below them.

"We can probably make it down there without being seen," Gabe said, "if we use the trees growing on the slope for cover as we make our way down."

"You are sure Likes Horses is there?"

Sees the Moon had put his finger on a point that had been bothering Gabe for some time. He had heard Camargo tell Rossiter that the Comancheros were heading home from Cinnabar City. But that didn't necessarily mean Likes Horses would still be with them. Nearly an entire day had passed since they and Rossiter had parted company. During that time, Camargo could easily have disposed of Likes Horses by selling her to someone along his route as he made his way back to the valley.

"No, I'm not sure for certain that she's down there," he told Sees the Moon. "But I'm hoping to hell she is. If she's not, well, I'll try to find out what they did with her and then—well, let's cross that bridge when we come to it, what do you say?"

"I say I am ready when you are."

"Let's go."

They moved cautiously down the steep slope of the hill, pursuing a zigzagging course that was dictated by the location of the trees behind which they took cover. When they finally reached the ranch, they crouched down close to the ground and listened to the sound of a woman singing inside the building that reached them through the open back door.

"I'm going to check the barn," Gabe said to Sees the Moon. "Maybe Camargo's got her locked up out there. Wait here for me."

He moved silently away, walking on the balls of his feet and maintaining his crouching position so as not to be seen

through either of the two windows at the rear wall of the
house. He rounded the corner of the building and from that
vantage point was able to see that no guard was stationed
outside the door of the barn. He looked around and, seeing no one in the area, loped across the distance that separated the barn from the house. He opened the barn door
and stepped inside. It took his eyes a moment to become
accustomed to the gloom of the barn's interior. When he
was able to see clearly, he realized that he was alone in the
building. Or so it seemed. To make sure that Likes Horses
was not in the barn, he checked all of the stalls and then
climbed the ladder to the hayloft. The stalls and the loft
were empty.

Once outside, he surveyed the area and then, keeping
one wary eye on the bunkhouse in the distance, loped back
the way he had come until he had rejoined Sees the Moon
behind the house.

"She's not in the barn," he told the Comanche. "There's
no activity out front. Maybe the Comancheros are off stealing somebody's cows."

At that moment, inside the house, a voice shouted, *"Bring
coffee!"*

Gabe recognized the voice as that of Miguel Camargo.
It had silenced the woman inside who had been singing.
Motioning to Sees the Moon to remain where he was, Gabe
flattened his back against the wall and eased up to the open
door. He removed his hat and then peered cautiously around
the door's jamb. He saw the Apache woman in the kitchen,
the one who apparently had been singing. She was the one
he had seen before when she served pancakes to him and
Camargo. She was busily engaged in making a pot of coffee, casting nervous glances at the door that led from the
kitchen to the rest of the house as she did so.

Gabe decided to take a chance on the plan he had just
conceived. It was based on the fact that the Apache woman
was probably not privy to the details of the Comancheros'
daily lives. If I'm right, he reasoned, she won't know that

I'm not riding with the Comancheros anymore. So . . .

He put his hat back on his head and boldly stepped through
the door into the kitchen. The Apache woman turned and,
at the unexpected sight of him, almost dropped the bag of
Arbuckle's coffee she had in her hands.

"I did not hear you come in, señor," she said in an unsteady
voice.

"Where's Camargo?" Gabe bluntly asked. "I've got to
see him."

"The padrone, he is in his bedroom, señor. With the
woman. I am to take coffee to them."

"Never mind about the coffee. I'll take it to them. But
first I've got to get my friend." Gabe went to the door and
beckoned.

Sees the Moon moved into the kitchen with a quizzical
expression on his face.

"Camargo's in the bedroom with Likes Horses," Gabe
told the Indian. "Since our business with him won't wait,
we're going to have to interrupt his little get-together."

Gabe picked up a dishcloth and used it to get a grip on
the hot metal handle of the coffeepot. "Is there anybody else
here in the house?" he asked the Apache woman, who was
standing nervously on the far side of the kitchen watching
him. "Besides you, I mean."

She shook her head.

"Come on," he said to Sees the Moon, and left the kitch-
en.

They made their way down the hall and stopped momentarily in front of an open door through which they could see
Camargo and Likes Horses. The Comanchero leader was
shirtless. He was sitting on the edge of the bed to which
Likes Horses was bound hand and foot as he prepared to pull
off his boots. There were scratches on his face and chest—
thin lines of coagulated blood that Gabe guessed were the
reason for Likes Horses being spread-eagled on her back and
tied to the bed. He drew from his waistband the revolver he
had confiscated from one of the guards in Cinnabar City

during the slave laborers' revolt, stepped into the room and announced in a falsely cheerful voice, "Coffee is served, sir."

Camargo froze in the act of pulling off his boot and stared in shock at Gabe and then at Sees the Moon, who stepped into the room behind Gabe with a gun in his hand as well. No words left the man's wildly working lips as he tried to speak. Surprise kept him dumb.

"Untie her," Gabe said to Sees the Moon.

Likes Horses managed a weak smile, her eyes on Gabe, as the Comanche moved toward the bed. "Long Rider," she breathed, relief lightening her voice.

Camargo put his foot down and stamped it down into his boot. He rose. Tried a smile that almost worked. "So we meet again, Conrad," he said, his voice emotionless but fire burning in his black eyes.

"I'm like the bad penny you've heard tell of," Gabe said. "I keep on turning up."

He saw Camargo's eyes shift to the gun belt draped over a chair next to the bed. "Don't go for it, Camargo," he warned. "I didn't come here to kill you but I will if I have to."

"You're a cold-blooded son of a bitch, Conrad."

"You're not so bad in the cold blood department yourself," Gabe countered, and then forcibly had to set Likes Horses aside as she, freed by Sees the Moon, sprang from the bed and threw her arms around him.

But he had made his move seconds too late. The instant Likes Horses had thrown herself upon him, Camargo had reached out and seized his gun.

As Likes Horses went stumbling backward away from Gabe as a result of his shove, Gabe threw the steaming contents of the pot he held in his hand in Camargo's direction.

The hot coffee showered the man's head and naked torso, causing him to scream shrilly and drop his weapon.

Sees the Moon quickly retrieved the dropped gun and backed toward the door of the room.

Gabe threw the empty coffeepot on the floor and took Likes Horses by the hand. "Adios, Camargo," he said, but was completely ignored by the badly burned man, who was turning in a tight circle in the center of the bedroom as he continued to scream and his burned flesh turned a bright red.

"Come on!" Gabe went running down the hall toward the kitchen with Likes Horses in tow and Sees the Moon right behind her. As they tore past the Apache woman, whose eyes were wide with alarm, and out the door into the bright sunlight, they almost ran right into the guns of Vickers and Sanchez, who were racing toward the house from their bunkhouse, and the one in the hand of Cuchillo, who had left his post atop the mesa.

"Sweet bleeding Jesus!" Vickers exclaimed when he caught sight of Gabe. "It's him again."

"Unkillable!" Sanchez exclaimed. "The man just can't be killed!"

"Do not shoot," Sees the Moon told the Comancheros as they stood in a tight group, their guns held steady in their hands. "You may kill us but we will also kill some of you before we die."

"What we got here it looks like to me," Vickers drawled, "is a Mexican standoff."

"We don't want a shoot-out," Gabe said quietly. "We just want to take Likes Horses and ride out of here."

"What did Camargo have to say about that?" Cuchillo asked. "We heard him scream so it is plain he did not like what you say you want to do."

Gabe noticed the slight shift in Cuchillo's gaze. The flicker in the man's eyes that meant—what? He wasn't sure, but what he had just seen made him decidedly uneasy. "Get behind me," he ordered Likes Horses, who promptly obeyed his order. "We're leaving now," he told the Comancheros, and took a step to the side. Sees the Moon did the same. "My gun's aimed straight at your gut, Cuchillo," he added, "so don't make a foolish move."

"*My* gun, it is aimed at your heart," Sees the Moon said in a chilly monotone to Vickers.

"But nobody's got a gun on me," Sanchez snapped as he squeezed off a shot that narrowly missed Sees the Moon.

Gabe was about to return the fire when he heard, "Don't shoot, Conrad!"

The voice—Camargo's voice—had come from behind Gabe.

"I've got a gun and its barrel is against the spine of the woman you came here to get."

Vickers giggled.

Gabe slowly turned around to face Camargo who, still shirtless, stood with his left arm around Likes Horses' throat and his gun against her back. One of Camargo's eyes was swollen shut from the burns he had suffered at Gabe's hands, and there were thick blisters forming on his exposed flesh.

So Camargo's what caught Cuchillo's eye a moment ago, Gabe thought. His gaze shifted when Camargo came out of the house behind me.

"Drop your guns," the Comanchero leader ordered.

Gabe dropped his gun. Sees the Moon dropped his.

"This time," Camargo began, staring at Gabe, "this time we will not hang you as we did before. This time we will not sell you as a slave laborer. This time I am going to put a bullet in your belly and then another one and then still another one until I have put enough bullets in you that you can do nothing but die. This time I will stay and watch until I am sure you are dead."

Gabe's eyes were on Likes Horses' face. Although he did not speak, he was trying to tell her not to be afraid, to be brave in the face of the danger they were confronting. She met his gaze and then seemed to straighten her stance despite Camargo's hold on her. Good, he thought. The girl's got guts.

"Stand over there, Conrad," Camargo ordered. "If I shoot you where you are now my rounds might go right through you and injure my men."

Gabe obediently stepped to the side. As he did so, Camargo let go of Likes Horses, who ran to Gabe and embraced him, her back to Camargo.

The Comanchero leader cursed under his breath. "Vickers, get that bitch away from Conrad. She's not for shooting. She's for selling."

"No!" Likes Horses cried, turning around to face Camargo with blazing eyes. "You will not sell me again. You will not—" She seemed to run out of words. Before Camargo knew what was happening, she had thrown herself upon him and shoved his gun aside as if it were a mere toy he was holding. She began to claw furiously at his face. At the same time she kicked him in the shins, not once but twice.

He let out a loud roar of rage and seized her by the throat with his free left hand and began squeezing.

Vickers giggled again. Sanchez and Cuchillo watched with interest as Camargo continued throttling Likes Horses.

Gabe lunged. But he never reached Camargo. Cuchillo brought the barrel of his gun down on the back of Gabe's neck. The blow dropped him to his knees.

He was on his way up again, determined to save Likes Horses and equally determined to kill Camargo, when the first of the Comanches appeared at the foot of the hill that rose behind the ranch. That man was followed by the others, who appeared from behind trees and boulders. All of them quickly advanced, the guns in their hands aimed at Camargo and his Comancheros. None of the Indians spoke. Their grim expressions said all there was to say.

"Where the hell did those redskins come from?" Sanchez blustered.

"They came from Cinnabar City with me," Gabe answered. "They're here to get even with you for what you did to them. Now, get rid of your guns and do it fast. If you move too slowly those redskins, as you seem pleased to call my friends—well, they're an impatient bunch, and they just might let light through you if you don't move fast enough to suit them."

The Comancheros wasted no time in getting rid of their guns.

"Camargo, you got some rope around here?" Gabe asked the Comanchero leader.

"Rope?" he repeated foolishly, unable to tear his eyes away from the threatening Comanches and their weapons.

"Take a look around," Gabe told Sees the Moon. "See if you can find some rope."

Minutes later, when the Indian returned with rope he had found in the barn, Gabe said, "Two of you go get four horses out of the corral and bring them back here."

By the time the two Indians Gabe had dispatched returned with four horses from the corral, he and Sees the Moon had fashioned nooses and had placed them around the necks of the four Comancheros after tying the men's hands behind their backs.

"Don't hang me, Conrad," Vickers pleaded. "Hanging, it's a helluva bad way to die. Show a man a little mercy, what do you say?"

"I don't intend to hang you, Vickers."

The Comanchero stared at him in disbelief. "But you put nooses around our necks! If that don't mean you're intend on having a necktie party, than what the Sam Hill does it mean?"

Instead of answering Vickers' question, Gabe gave instructions to several of the Comanches, who promptly proceeded to manhandle the four Comancheros up onto the bare backs of the horses that had been brought from the corral. Then they looped the free ends of the four ropes over the branch of a tree growing in front of the house.

"He's a liar, Conrad is," Camargo snarled. "He says he doesn't intend to hang us and yet he's got us strung up here—"

"*I* don't intend to hang you, Camargo. You and your boys, though, might wind up hanging yourselves."

"What the hell—" Camargo began, but then fell silent as Gabe glared at him.

When the Comanches had finished tying the free ends of the four ropes to the trunk of the tree, Gabe said, "We're leaving now."

"You're leaving?" Sanchez asked, incredulity in his eyes.

"You're leaving us strung up here like this?" an equally incredulous Cuchillo asked.

"Somebody might show up at any minute and cut you boys down," Gabe declared. "Then again maybe nobody will show up for days. In that case, you'll just have to be patient and sit nice and still in your saddles so that you don't make a false move and wind up hanging yourselves."

"You can't leave us here like this," Vickers protested.

"You're wrong, Vickers. I damn well can and I fully intend to. Which is better treatment than you gave me when you put a noose around *my* neck. As I recall, you ran my horse out from under me and then rode off and left me swinging. Hell, what I've just had done to you, it's downright humane compared to your treatment of me. Not to mention your friend Camargo's treatment of Likes Horses while she was unlucky enough to be in his hands. And last, but by no means least, what I've had done to you—it's the very soul of charity compared to selling people like cattle to the highest bidders."

"Wait!" Camargo called out as Gabe beckoned and Likes Horses and the other Comanches began to follow him as he headed for the hill rising behind the ranch. "I'll make a deal with you, Conrad! A *good* deal."

Gabe ignored him and thrust his revolver back into his waistband as he began to climb the hill.

When the party reached the top of the hill, they all turned to look down into the valley.

Camargo and his men sat virtually motionless on their horses, their frightened eyes gazing upward to where Gabe and the others stood on the ridge watching them.

Likes Horses suddenly moved away from Gabe's side and collided with Sees the Moon, causing the man to drop his gun, which fired when it hit the ground.

The sound of the report roared through the valley, startling the Comancheros' horses and causing them to bolt.

Camargo and his Comancheros were jerked off the backs of the fleeing horses to hang suspended in mid-air. They slowly twisted at the ends of the ropes around their broken necks, their eyes bulging out of their sockets and their tongues protruding from their mouths.

Gabe's eyes drifted to Likes Horses.

She met his penetrating gaze and said simply, "I slipped. It was an accident."

He nodded, not believing for a minute that her collision with Sees the Moon was an accident, and said, "Let's go. We've got a long ride ahead of us."

They arrived at Chief Ten Bears' village the following day. A happy uproar greeted them. People ran to meet them as they rode in. Friends and relatives of the Comanche men embraced them, kissed them and hugged them as if they would never let them go again. There were shouts of joy and much laughter. A dog ran around and around the reunited group, barking and vigorously wagging its tail as if it too were welcoming the returned captives.

Gabe and Likes Horses dismounted and watched the reunion, neither of them speaking. Then, as Chief Ten Bears appeared on the far side of the village and his people hailed him and gleefully announced the return of those the Apaches had captured, he began to make his way toward them.

"There will be feasting tonight," Likes Horses told Gabe. "The drums will speak. There will be dancing."

He nodded. "Your grandfather looks real pleased to see you again."

"And I am so glad to see him again," Likes Horses cried. Without another word, she left Gabe and went running to meet her grandfather.

Gabe watched as the two embraced, and tears welled in the chief's eyes and slid down his weathered cheeks. Over Likes Horses' shoulder, Ten Bears gazed at Gabe and called

out, "Thank you, Long Rider." Then he held his granddaughter out at arm's length, his smile widening as he gazed
lovingly at her.

Nearby, Sees the Moon was wrapped in the embrace of
a young woman who planted kiss after happy kiss on his
face as he beamed happily at Gabe.

The other young men talked eagerly of what had happened to them. Their friends and relatives listened in awe
and wonder to their tales.

My job here's done, Gabe thought as he continued to
watch the happy homecoming. It's time I was moving on.

As he put a foot in a stirrup, he heard Likes Horses say,
"Long Rider was wonderful, Grandfather, truly wonderful."
As he swung into the saddle, he heard her add, "You should
have seen how he—" Then he could hear her no more as
her voice was drowned out by other voices just as joyful
as hers.

Minutes later, holding her grandfather by the hand, she
turned, smiling broadly, and called out, "Long Rider—"

But Gabe was gone.

A special offer for people who enjoy reading the best
Westerns published today. If you enjoyed this book,
subscribe now and get . . .

TWO FREE

A $5.90 VALUE—NO OBLIGATION

If you enjoyed this book and would like to read more of the very best Westerns being published today, you'll want to subscribe to True Value's Western Home Subscription Service. If you enjoyed the book you just read and want more of the most exciting, adventurous, action packed Westerns, subscribe now.

Each month the editors of True Value will select the 6 very best Westerns from America's leading publishers for special readers like you. You'll be able to preview these new titles as soon as they are published, FREE for ten days with no obligation.

TWO FREE BOOKS

When you subscribe, we'll send you your first month's shipment of the newest and best 6 Westerns for you to preview. With your first shipment, two of these books will be yours as our introductory gift to you absolutely FREE, regardless of what you decide to do. If you like them, as much as we think you will, keep all six books but pay for just 4 at the low subscriber rate of just $2.45 each. If you decide to return them, keep 2 of the titles as our gift. No obligation.

Special Subscriber Savings

When you become a True Value subscriber you'll save money several ways. First, all regular monthly selections will be billed at the low subscriber price of just $2.45 each. That's

WESTERNS!

at least a savings of $3.00 each month below the publishers price. Second, there is never any shipping, handling or other hidden charges—Free home delivery. What's more there is no minimum number of books you must buy, you may return any selection for full credit and you can cancel your subscription at any time. A TRUE VALUE!

Mail the coupon below

To start your subscription and receive 2 FREE WESTERNS, fill out the coupon below and mail it today. We'll send your first shipment which includes 2 FREE BOOKS as soon as we receive it.